MORGAN'S MERCENARIES
MAVERICK HEARTS
III

*"Rafe Antonio at your service,
Señorita Worthington."*

As his strong mouth grazed Ari's hand, a wild series of shocks leapt up her arm. No one had ever kissed her hand before! But the minute Rafe raised his head, she saw that his brown eyes were hard and merciless looking.

"Ohh...well...thank you, Señor Antonio...." She quickly pulled her hand away.

"Call me Rafe," he told her. He didn't want to like her. He couldn't bear to think of spending the coming months keeping guard over a woman— especially a woman like this.

But Morgan Trayhern was counting on him. And Rafe wasn't the kind of man who would shirk his duty.

D005084

Dear Reader,

During the warm days of July, what better way to kick back and enjoy the best of summer reading than with six stellar stories from Special Edition as we continue to celebrate Silhouette's 20th Anniversary all year long!

With *The Pint-Sized Secret*, Sheryl Woods continues to delight her readers with another winning installment of her popular miniseries AND BABY MAKES THREE: THE DELACOURTS OF TEXAS. Reader favorite Lindsay McKenna starts her new miniseries, MORGAN'S MERCENARIES: MAVERICK HEARTS, with *Man of Passion*, her fiftieth book. A stolen identity leads to true love in Patricia Thayer's compelling *Whose Baby Is This?* And a marriage of convenience proves to be anything but in rising star Allison Leigh's *Married to a Stranger* in her MEN OF THE DOUBLE-C RANCH miniseries. Rounding off the month is celebrated author Pat Warren's *Doctor and the Debutante*, where the healthy dose of romance is just what the physician ordered, while for the heroine in Beth Henderson's *Maternal Instincts*, a baby-sitting assignment turns into a practice run for motherhood—and marriage.

Hope you enjoy this book and the other unforgettable stories Special Edition is happy to bring you this month!

All the best,

Karen Taylor Richman,
Senior Editor

Please address questions and book requests to:
Silhouette Reader Service
U.S.: 3010 Walden Ave., P.O. Box 1325, Buffalo, NY 14269
Canadian: P.O. Box 609, Fort Erie, Ont. L2A 5X3

LINDSAY McKENNA
MAN OF PASSION

SPECIAL EDITION®

Published by Silhouette Books

America's Publisher of Contemporary Romance

If you purchased this book without a cover you should be aware
that this book is stolen property. It was reported as "unsold and
destroyed" to the publisher, and neither the author nor the
publisher has received any payment for this "stripped book."

To Karen David, a delightful maverick in her own right,
and a dear friend

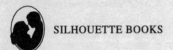 SILHOUETTE BOOKS

ISBN 0-373-24334-0

MAN OF PASSION

Copyright © 2000 by Lindsay McKenna

All rights reserved. Except for use in any review, the reproduction
or utilization of this work in whole or in part in any form by any
electronic, mechanical or other means, now known or hereafter
invented, including xerography, photocopying and recording, or in
any information storage or retrieval system, is forbidden without
the written permission of the editorial office, Silhouette Books,
300 East 42nd Street, New York, NY 10017 U.S.A.

All characters in this book have no existence outside the imagination of
the author and have no relation whatsoever to anyone bearing the same
name or names. They are not even distantly inspired by any individual
known or unknown to the author, and all incidents are pure invention.

This edition published by arrangement with Harlequin Books S.A.

® and TM are trademarks of Harlequin Books S.A., used under license.
Trademarks indicated with ® are registered in the United States Patent
and Trademark Office, the Canadian Trade Marks Office and in other
countries.

Visit Silhouette at www.eHarlequin.com

Printed in U.S.A.

Books by Lindsay McKenna

LINDSAY McKENNA

is a practicing homeopath and emergency medical technician on the Navajo Reservation. She lives with her husband, David, near Sedona.

Dear Reader,

I'm just as much in love with Morgan Trayhern and his brave men and women who work at Perseus as you are! And after hearing how much you loved my last series, MORGAN'S MERCENARIES: THE HUNTERS, I wanted to find out what Morgan was up to next!

Morgan's mercenaries tend to be alpha men and women warriors—mavericks who don't quite fit into society. In the spirit of the maverick, I decided to write about three men who broke the mold when they were born in MORGAN'S MERCENARIES: MAVERICK HEARTS.

Rafe Antonio, the hero of *Man of Passion,* comes from a very rich and noble background, but by turning his back on what his family expects of him, he has severely disappointed his father, the owner of a banking empire in Manaus, Brazil. In South America, the firstborn male of any family is expected to learn the family business and take it over when the father tells the son to do so. But the mysterious Amazon Basin calls to Rafe. That is why he takes the lowly job of a backwoodsman, or forest ranger, working to protect the Indian people.

Arianna Worthington is a young woman who is trying to find herself. More than anything, Ari wants to fulfill her deceased mother's last wish. But to do so, she must go against her powerful father and head for the Amazon. When she meets Rafe, she never expects to fall in love. And neither does he....

I'm celebrating a special milestone with this book—it is my fiftieth for Silhouette! Hope you enjoy reading it as much as I did writing it.

Sincerely,

Lindsay McKenna

Chapter One

"Morgan, I'm glad you could make it," Ben Worthington said, standing up from behind his large cherry desk and thrusting his square hand out toward him.

"Ben, it's been awhile since we saw one another," Morgan replied. Grasping the secretary of the Navy's hand firmly, he saw Ben's blue eyes narrow with concern, and wondered once again what had prompted his old friend's sudden invitation.

"Have a seat," Ben invited. "Becky," he called to his assistant, who sat in the outer office, "is the coffee on the way?"

Morgan took a seat in the leather wing chair at the corner of Worthington's desk and looked around the spacious Pentagon office. All kinds of Navy memorabilia—paintings, photos, diplomas—were affixed to the walls. Ben had been a Navy pilot on the carrier *Enterprise* during the Vietnam War. Ben's desk looked just as cluttered and busy as his own, Morgan thought. Through the venetian blinds Morgan could see a patch of blue sky and fluffy white clouds. It was spring in Washington, D.C., and hundreds of cherry trees with white perfumed blossoms surrounded the Capitol and nearby monuments.

As Worthington's prim and brisk secretary entered the office, silver tray in hand, Morgan gave her a nod. She smiled and handed him a white china cup decorated in gold trim.

"If I remember right, Mr. Trayhern, you like your coffee straight?"

Grinning, Morgan took the proffered cup and saucer. "Indeed I do, Becky. You've got a long memory."

She smiled broadly and gave her boss his coffee. "Details are important around here, as you know, sir." She set the tray on a cherry coffee table that sat off to one side, near the cream-colored, buttery-soft leather sofa. "And in case either of you wants a midmorning snack, there's a delicious coffee cake drizzled with caramel just begging to be eaten."

Groaning, Morgan thanked the tall, graceful secretary, whose red hair had become peppered with silver since he'd last seen her. In her mid-fifties, Becky had been working for Ben Worthington for a long time, and she was more than just an assistant, she was his right hand.

"I need that coffee cake like I need a hole in my head," Morgan confided to Ben as Becky quietly closed the door to the office to leave them in complete privacy.

Ben raised his thick, sandy-colored brows as he sipped his coffee. "Makes two of us. I don't get out and exercise like I used to." He looked around the office. "Maybe it's this place."

"Or the pressures and crises that keep popping up to throw you off your scheduled maintenance," Morgan said, his mouth twisted wryly.

"I see you know that one, too."

"My middle name is crisis," Morgan agreed with a chuckle. He eyed the coffee cake. "I shouldn't, but I'm going to...." Rising to his full height, he unbuttoned his dark blue pinstripe jacket and moved over to the coffee table. Twisting to look over his shoulder at Ben, he asked, "Want to join me in collusion?"

Laughing, Ben patted his girth. "I'm twenty pounds over right now, Morgan. I don't dare."

"I just thought I'd have some company so I wouldn't feel so guilty about cutting such a huge piece for myself," he murmured as he sliced off a healthy portion and placed it on a china plate. Picking up the plate along with one of the forks and white linen napkins Becky had thoughtfully left behind, Morgan moved back to the wing chair and sat down.

"What's on your mind, Ben?"

Scowling, Ben put his coffee aside and picked up

one of several gold-framed photographs on one side of his massive desk. "How long have we known one another?"

Morgan sat back and chewed on the sweet, mouth-melting coffee cake. "Almost as long as Perseus has been in existence," he replied, referring to the covert government organization he headed.

Moving his hands over one small photo, Ben studied it. "That was ten years ago. Arianna was only fourteen years old when you formed Perseus." He looked up. "She's my youngest of three children." Turning the photo around, he placed it so that Morgan could get a good look at her.

"Pretty young lady," Morgan commented. The photograph showed a woman of perhaps twenty-four or -five sitting among a number of potted plants in a greenhouse. She was delicate looking, with short, blond hair and her father's sky blue eyes in an oval face. She was dressed in a pair of jeans, a pink tank top and tennis shoes. The expression on her face was one of pure joy.

Ben leaned back in his chair, his hands folded across his belly. "Arianna was only eight when her mother died of leukemia. She was the youngest and it was very hard on her. She was too young to understand…and her mother's death changed her forever…. I tried to help, but I was hurting so much myself that I'm afraid I didn't do a very good job of being a parent at that time…."

Morgan lost some of his joviality as Ben turned another framed photograph around for him to look at. It showed Ben and his wife, Ellen. "I'm sorry for your loss," he murmured sincerely. In some respects, Ellen reminded him of his own wife, Laura, who also had blond hair. "Arianna really takes after your wife, doesn't she?"

"In *every* respect," Ben muttered. "Which is why I asked you to drop by and see me." Ben waved his hand. "I know you have other appointments today, equally important, and I'm grateful you could squeeze this impromptu visit into your schedule."

Morgan finished the tasty coffee cake. He blotted his lips with the napkin and picked up the cup of coffee. "I'm glad I could do it. I gather this involves something personal instead of professional?"

Ben sat for a moment, his square face stern, his jowls set, his gaze pinned on his daughter's photograph. Rousing himself, he nodded. "Yes…it concerns Arianna. And what she thinks she's about to do."

Morgan heard the pain in the man's somber voice and sympathized, though he had a feeling he knew what was bothering him. Ben was a hard-hitting Type A personality—a born leader, who liked to control every nuance of his life. As secretary of the Navy, his commanding leadership was a good thing. But Morgan wondered how Ben's controlling personality might have impacted his family. He'd seen too many military men who were far too rigid with their wife and children.

"Fill me in on how I can help you," Morgan said.

Ben sighed and picked up the picture of his daughter, holding it as he spoke. "Arianna is so much like her mother that since she's grown up, I sometimes forget and think Ellen's in the town house whenever Arianna comes over. Arianna's twenty-five now, and has just graduated from Georgetown University with a degree in business and a minor in Spanish."

"Impressive," Morgan murmured. He thought of his own children, who were growing up quickly. Jason was ten now, and little Katy wasn't far behind. And the fraternal twins, Peter and Kelly, were a year old. "I've got a college fund already established for my four kids. I'm hoping they'll see the benefits of a college education like your daughter, Arianna, has."

Worthington's mouth tightened slightly. "I forced her into getting a degree in business. Maybe it was wrong of me, but I wanted Ari to have a solid foundation, so she could earn money and control her own life instead of having it controlled by others. She's a very intelligent girl, if she'd just settle down."

Touching the frame, Ben continued unhappily, "She's a dreamer, not a hard-core business type, Morgan. My wife was a dreamer, too. Lord, she had so many dreams. Ellen loved to travel. She wanted to go around the world. She loved orchids, and I had a small greenhouse built for her. Ellen and Arianna spent hours out in that little steamy box where she grew all those orchids. In fact, the year before Ellen died, she made a concerted effort to be with Arianna. They spent a couple hours every day, up until the last two weeks before her death, out in that greenhouse.''

Touched, Morgan murmured, ''It was a parting gift of love that Ellen gave to her then.''

Ben's normally hard face softened somewhat. ''Yes…Ari was all she had left. Our son, Kirk, was at the Naval Academy at the time.'' He gave Morgan a pained look. ''I think you already know our middle daughter, Janis, died at age thirteen. She took a stupid dare from a boy at a riding stable. He bet that the horse she was riding couldn't jump a four-foot fence. It didn't, and she fell off and broke her neck, dying instantly. It was a blow to all of us, but especially Ellen.'' Rubbing his neck, Ben muttered, ''I sometimes think that the shock of her death—the trauma of our loss—triggered Ellen's leukemia. She contracted the disease six months after Janis died. It's too coincidental, in my book.''

''And Ari got shunted aside during that time?''

''Yes, but she was the kind of little girl who would go off to her room and play for hours in a make-believe world.'' Ben roused himself and gave Morgan a half smile. ''She still does. And that's the problem.''

''How?''

''One of the things my wife wanted to do more than anything else was take a trip down to the Amazon in Brazil to find orchids and draw them. My wife had a master's degree in art. She was an incredible artist. She talked to Ari endlessly about all her dreams, and urged her to fill her life with exploration, with adventure, with going places.''

''All the places Ellen hadn't gotten to go, right?''

''Yes.'' Grimly, Ben sat up and said, ''Ari has it in her head to go down to Brazil, to that damned jungle, and do exactly as her mother said—find orchids, draw them and have a book published on them. The only problem is that Ari is a delicate child. She hasn't got any backbone. She's painfully shy and has low self-esteem. Yet,'' Ben growled in frustration, ''she wants to traipse off to Brazil and do this crazy, stupid thing.''

''She's twenty-five,'' Morgan said. ''Old enough to make up her mind on what she wants to do.''

''That's the point!'' Ben shot out of the chair and began to pace, his hands resting on his hips. ''Ari has been a good girl. She's been responsible. She's done everything I've ever asked of her. Then, all of a sudden, she comes for a visit and tells me—*tells me*—that she wants to fulfill this crazy dream for her mother.''

''Why not let her?'' Morgan asked. He could easily understand what was fueling the daughter's rebellion. In making her mother's dying wish come true, she would help to heal herself from the loss of her beloved parent.

''Because,'' Ben said, turning and glaring at Morgan, ''she's not an artist! She has no degree in art. Oh, she dabbles with her colored pencils, and her mother did teach her some art techniques…but to think that she's got the kind of artistic professionalism that a book demands? No. No way. I just don't want to see her set herself up for disappointment. And risk her neck by running around a foreign country alone.''

Ben sighed. ''Ellen used to read Arianna books on Brazil. They would sit for hours with five or six orchid books spread all across her bed, and they'd make plans about which species should be drawn for the book. Ari has it in her head that she can go gallivanting off to the jungle and draw those orchids.''

Shrugging, Morgan finished the coffee and said, ''I haven't met a twenty-something yet who didn't rebel, didn't want to go out and knock heads with life, Ben. If this is her rebellion, I'd say it's a pretty healthy one, from my perspective.''

''Don't side with her on this,'' Ben warned. ''There're drug runners down in Manaus. There's as much cocaine being funneled up through that country as there is rainwater pouring down on the Amazon jungle. I'm worried about her. She's been a homebody. She's not an explorer. She's not worldly or even practical, Morgan.''

''In other words, Ari needs a baby-sitter and a guard dog? Is that why you asked to see me? You want me to assign a merc to her while she's down there, to keep her out of trouble?''

''Out of harm's way,'' Ben added fiercely. He raked his fingers through his short, neatly cut hair. Sitting down, he sighed. ''Ari is a mouse, Morgan. She's a shadow. She *clung* to Ellen. She was afraid to do anything unless Ellen cajoled her into it. Ari was happy to stay at home, work with my wife on the orchids, be in the greenhouse with her. She doesn't have the drive my son or I have. She doesn't have a game plan for her life. Ari goes around in this idealistic, spacy kind of state, believing good of everyone and everything. She's too damned trusting. Too forgiving.''

Sighing, Morgan said, "Life has a way of giving us more backbone, more reality-based perspectives, Ben. But to get that, you have to go out of the home and through life's revolving doors into the fray we call the real world. You know that. It sounds like Ari is ready to do it. I don't see that as bad, do you?''

"Why the hell couldn't she just take the job I got her on Wall Street? I have a major stock brokerage firm that wants her right this minute. But she said no. She wants to take a year off, go to the Amazon and draw orchids and create this book. Hell, it'll fail. She'll fail.''

"Failing is a part of living," Morgan said. "Failing gives us strength, endurance and backbone." When Ben's face flushed with anger, he held up his hand. "I think I've got just the man for this personal mission to protect Arianna from herself.''

"Who is he?'' Ben demanded, getting up again. He poured himself more coffee and filled Morgan's cup while he was at it.

"Name's Rafe Antonio. He's what they call a *mateiro* or a backwoodsman, in Brazil. In our country, he'd be known as a forest ranger. He has a territory about three hours east of Manaus, down the Amazon

River, that he protects from poachers, miners and drug runners. His main care is for the Indians in that region. He's a good man, Ben. Someone you can trust.''

"And you've worked with him before?"

"Many times. Antonio is a mole in the Brazilian government for Perseus. He's aided us on a number of missions over the years. He's also our eyes and ears down there regarding the drug trade."

"And how do you think he'll react to having to baby-sit my daughter?"

"I don't know," Morgan said. "I'll contact him and find out. Rafe is someone you want around if trouble stirs. He comes from a very rich, old, aristocratic family in Manaus. His father's family comes from direct Castilian Spain aristocracy. His mother was a socialite from São Paulo. Senor Antonio is a very rich and powerful man in Brazil."

"Sounds like Rafe went his own way," Ben muttered. "If he comes from rich and successful parents, not to mention aristocratic bloodlines, to be nothing more than a damned forest ranger—"

"Hold on," Morgan warned. "Rafe has a Ph.D. in biology from Stanford Medical University in California. He's written several books on herbs used by the medicine men and women down in the Amazon Basin. He's widely regarded as an expert on them by scientific and pharmaceutical industries around the world."

"Oh," Ben muttered, "I thought he was just a junkyard dog."

"With no breeding and papers?" Morgan controlled his mounting anger. Sometimes Ben Worthington was a snob. He was born of money, power and position, and had not come up through the ranks of the little people, as Morgan had.

"All right, all right. I was out of line. I apologize. So you think he can handle my daughter?"

"Rafe won't 'handle' your daughter," Morgan said softly. "I'll give him orders to protect her, though, to help her fulfill her mother's dream. He lives on a houseboat three hours from Manaus. I'm sure he can provide shelter for Ari."

"Frankly, I'd like him to talk my bullheaded daughter into coming straight home."

"You aren't going to be able to tell a twenty-five-year-old much," Morgan said with a chuckle.

Ben scowled heavily and drummed his fingers on the desk. "Tell this Antonio that if he talks my daughter into doing an about-face at Manaus International Airport, there's a hundred thousand dollar bonus in it for him."

Morgan hesitated. "I'm afraid that kind of carrot dangling in front of Rafe won't work. He's got pretty strong moral and ethical boundaries. He can't be bought off, Ben."

"You mean he wouldn't try and talk my daughter into turning around and getting back on a plane headed for the States?"

Morgan shook his head. "He's a man of honor. The type of honor the old Castilian aristocracy still has. Actually, he should be living in Victorian, or maybe Napoleonic times. He's fighting for the underdogs, the weak, and those who need the kind of help he can supply. The miners, drug runners and drug lords hate him and have a heavy price out on his head. Rafe is a modern-day knight in many respects. I don't think he would take money to do something he saw as underhanded to someone like Arianna.''

Snorting, Ben rolled his eyes skyward. "Just my luck."

"I choose people with strong morals and values, Ben. You know that. If they aren't in that category, Perseus won't hire them."

"I know, I know...." he said in exasperation. "On one hand, I feel good he'll protect Ari. On the other...well, dammit, everyone can be bought for a price. It just depends upon what's important to them. Does he have a foundation or something set up for his Indians?"

"Yes, he does." Morgan eyed him warily. "If you think a hefty donation to his foundation will make him talk Ari out of staying in the Amazon to complete her dream, you're barking up the wrong tree, Ben. In this case, Ari is the underdog and Rafe won't take your side against her at any price."

"Just a thought..." Ben leaned back in his chair, pondering the situation. "Well, I've got one last chance to talk Ari out of this fiasco adventure of hers. I swear, she's like Joan of Arc on a mission. I've never seen her like this. Before...well, she did what I wanted or asked of her. Now she's digging in her heels like some kind of fanatical zealot and refusing to budge from her position. This is a girl who always knew the meaning of the word *compromise* and would bend over backwards for me." Drumming his fingers again, he added in a frustrated tone, "But not this time."

Sitting up, Morgan said gently, "Ben, maybe your daughter needs to spread her wings. She's at that age. I watch our kids growing up, and every day I see them becoming more and more independent from us."

Arching one brow, Ben said, "And you encourage it?"

"Of course. The last thing Laura and I want are kids who can't struggle and survive in life. They have to learn how to do that. It hurts us to see Jason and Katy exploring, knowing that they're going to make a mistake, or learn a hard lesson. No denying it's painful to watch. But they've *got* to make mistakes, Ben. You can't keep protecting Ari because you lost your other daughter. And reading between the lines, it looks like you did just that and she's become very dependent upon you as a result." Opening his hands, his voice becoming softer, Morgan added, "Loving our kids is hell on our hearts, Ben. And with you losing Ellen, as well as Janis... well, I can't blame you for wanting to protect Ari like you have. Someday I'm sure she'll appreciate what you've done and are trying to do for her."

"But not now?"

"She's only twenty-five," Morgan said, smiling

faintly. "Remember when you were in your twenties, Ben?"

"Yeah, I had a jet strapped to my butt and I was shooting Migs out of the skies over North Vietnam."

"Not exactly a safe job, was it? Did you ever think what your parents must have felt or thought?"

"Not at the time, no. I felt it was my right to do what I wanted to do."

"Okay…then transfer that feeling, that driving need to be yourself, to Ari. That's where she's at."

"Humph."

Morgan drank his coffee and allowed his words to sink in. He saw Ben's large, fleshy features set into a bulldog look of denial. Placing his cup on its saucer, Morgan said, "At least she hasn't got a jet strapped to her, out in combat. Look at the bright side of this. Hunting down orchids and sketching them isn't exactly dangerous. Let her off that protective leash you've got her on. Rafe Antonio is a man of honor. A modern-day knight. I know he'll care for Ari like you or I would, if we were in his shoes."

"But…she's just a girl!"

"Maybe you need to shift how you see Ari," Morgan warned. "At twenty-five, Ari is no 'girl.' She's a young woman."

Rubbing his brow fiercely, Ben glowered across the desk. "Dammit, Morgan, did Ari pay *you* to come in here and be on *her* side of this thing?"

Grinning sourly, Morgan sipped his coffee. "Not a chance, Ben. This is a parent talking to a parent.

Jason's ten. In three years he'll hit his teens, and from what I'm seeing, he's going to be a rebel without a cause. A handful. At least Ari is rebelling for the *right* reasons. She wants closure with her mother's death and maybe she hopes to find herself—her *real* self—without any of her family being around. All kids need that adventure in life to give them a sense of who they really are. Ari needs to find out who *she* is. Not the daughter. Not the sister. But herself.''

''I should pay you a hundred bucks an hour to be my shrink,'' Ben griped good-naturedly.

Chuckling, Morgan stood up. ''I'm going to be late for my appointment with the Joint Chiefs of Staff if I don't hightail it out of here, Ben.'' He thrust his hand out to his old friend. ''I'll have my office fax a dossier on Rafe Antonio, and his photo, to you. You'll have them by this afternoon. That way, you can talk intelligently with your daughter about him being her guide.''

''Bodyguard.''

Morgan released Ben's hand. ''That, too. My office will get in touch with Rafe by Iridium phone satellite transmission. Down there in the jungle, only direct satellite transmissions can get info in and out. Standard cell phones are useless. I'll make sure my people give you the confirmation that he knows Ari is coming to Manaus. Just call and give them the airline and flight information.''

Ben sighed and looked dejectedly down at his desk. ''I don't know, Morgan. Being a parent is hell.

I worry for Ari. I'll probably have insomnia while she's down there...."

"When you read up on Antonio, I don't think you'll lose sleep," Morgan reassured him as he opened the door. "Just tell Ari she's in good hands."

Chapter Two

"Will you settle down?" Ari hissed the words to herself as she sat tensely in the living room of her condo. It was located near Georgetown University, where she'd spent five years of her life pursuing a degree she didn't want. Her father was to meet her at 8:00 p.m. She knew he'd be punctual; he always was. In fact, he ran his life by that darned appointment book of his. After all, Ben Worthington was a power broker who moved in the highest circles of politics and government in the country.

Chewing on her full lower lip—a nervous habit she took up whenever she was about to have a confrontation with him or anyone—she uncrossed her legs and sat straight on the flowery print couch. Her mind raced. She had to have all the reasons why she had to go to the Amazon down pat or her father would shred them with his cold, analytical skills. Her heart almost burst with anticipation and she collapsed against the back of the couch. She *had* to go! Her father *had* to let her.

When the doorbell rang, Ari jumped what felt like three feet off the couch. Instantly, her stomach knotted as she leaped to her feet and walked breathlessly to the door, smoothing a hand over the long-sleeved lavender blouse she wore with dark navy trousers and comfortable brown loafers. Opening the door, she saw her father standing there, towering over her with his massive height. She could see dark shadows beneath his pale blue eyes, and the set of his mouth sent a frisson of fear through her. Beneath his left arm was a manila envelope, and he carried a black leather briefcase.

"Hi, Father, come on in…." She stepped aside. "You look really tired. Hard day?"

Ben ambled into the small, neatly kept condo. "It was a tough day, Ari. Yes, I'm beat." He glanced around the room, realizing once again how much her condo reflected Ellen's taste in furniture, colors and greenery. Ari had created space for about six orchids on the windowsills. Some of them were in bloom. When he halted, turned and looked down at his youngest daughter, he thought about how much she looked like Ellen had when they'd first gotten married. They'd been in their mid-twenties, and Ben recalled vividly how he'd plunged over the edge when he'd seen Ellen. She was so alive, almost ethereal.

More like a diaphanous cloud than something created from terra firma. Though Ari had his light blue eyes, she had Ellen's thick, gold hair and oval face. In fact, Ari was the same height and build as Ellen. His daughter had let her hair grow since graduating from college and it hung in a loose pageboy around her slumped shoulders.

Ben wished Ari would square her shoulders and stand up tall and proud. But she never did. He watched as she fluttered around the living room, removing several magazines from the couch to the coffee table, next to the lacy fern that sat there.

"Have you eaten?" Ari asked, her heart pounding hard with anxiety.

"Yes, I have." Ben sat down. Ari took the overstuffed chair opposite him. Chewing on her lip, she watched as her father put down the briefcase and then slowly opened the thick manila envelope.

"What's that?" She hoped it was her airline ticket for Manaus.

"Your adventure," he muttered. Lifting his head, his hand resting on the papers he placed on his lap, he said, "Are you *sure* you want to do this, Ari? I've got a job on Wall Street waiting for you. Why can't you drop this idea of yours and do something solid for your career?"

Hurt wove through her. She avoided his piercing blue gaze. Ari had a tough time looking people squarely in the eyes. She always felt so worthless, so inept and small in comparison to those who could boldly meet someone's gaze and hold it. She admired people who could. She felt like a coward most of the time. Rubbing her face with her hands, she whispered, "Father, I've *got* to do this!" Her soft voice grew fervent. "Please? This is for Mom." She put her hand against her heart. "She dreamed so much of going to the Amazon to hunt orchids and draw them. I really want to do this for her."

Wearily, Ben studied his daughter's features in the lamplight. She looked more girl than woman to him. Maybe Morgan was right and he needed to see Ari differently. But dammit, it was hard. Almost impossible to do. "But you can't even draw, Ari!" Instantly, he saw how his words wounded her. Every little emotion registered across her face, just as it had on Ellen's. They were so much alike that it broke his heart. "I'm sorry, Ari…you just don't have your mother's education and training. You never took a course in art."

Pressing both hands to her heart, Ari fought back the tears. She felt like such a loser. She wanted desperately to please her father, but this *thing,* this urge deep in her heart and gut, was driving her like a fanatical force that would no longer be ignored. She *had* to respond to it, to how she really felt. Heart aching, Ari whispered, "I know I'm a lousy artist, Father. I don't even pretend to call myself one. But I love to sketch. I used to sketch with Mom all the time. Remember how she'd loan me some of her paper and colored pencils and we'd both draw the orchid she chose?"

"Only too well," Ben admitted tiredly. On the

walls of Ari's condo were at least ten of Ellen's orig-
inal paintings of her beloved orchids. Ellen had been
a small sensation in the art world with her talent for
portraying the luscious, feminine-looking orchids. It
had started as a hobby, but she had eventually made
a lot of money at it, as well as achieving no small
amount of fame.

Ben studied Ari. She looked helpless to him, her
hands pressed against her small breasts, her eyes
pleading. What tore at him most were the unshed
tears he saw in them. Dammit, he didn't mean to
hurt her or make her cry. Ellen would cry at anything
and everything. Ari was no different.

"Look," he said gruffly, "I've got your airline
ticket here, your passport and everything you need.
You're going, okay?"

Instantly, Ben saw a shining, joyous light come to
her large, widening eyes.

"Oh, thank you, Father!" Ari leaped off the chair,
came around the coffee table and threw her arms
around his neck, giving him a fierce hug.

"Ari...don't get carried away," he ordered
brusquely, untangling his daughter's arms from
around his neck. "You're not a little kid anymore,"
he muttered. "You're a young woman...."

Laughing delightedly, Ari sat there, one leg beneath her on the couch as she felt a thrill of freedom
flow through her. He was going to let her go to Manaus! Suddenly she was scared. She'd lived with fear
all her life, so this was just a new kind to her. It felt
delicious in comparison to her other fears, however.

Soaring giddily on the news, she said, "Father, are you saying I'm too old to give you a hug every now and then?" He had always been uncomfortable with touching and holding, and Ari never understood why. Her mother had been such a toucher and hugger in comparison, but Ari had never seen her parents kiss or even hold hands out in public. Yet she knew to this day that her dad still loved her mother fiercely. Her photos were everywhere in his condominium and on his desk at the Pentagon. Ari knew he kept a color photo of her mother in his wallet, too.

"You're growing into a young woman," he said bluntly. "You and I have to adjust to that." He hoped by using Morgan's words that he could help Ari feel a little more confident about herself. A little more sure. Ben had never seen such a flighty, uncertain person as Ari. He blamed it on the unexpected death of Janis and then her mother. Despite their age difference, Ari and Janis had been very close. And Ari had almost given up on living after Janis died. She was just a shadow, no, a mouse who ducked and dodged her way through life, running to the safety of her dream world.

Trying to quiet her spontaneous outburst, because she knew her father disapproved of effusive emotional displays—touching him with her hand or, heaven forbid, hugging him around the neck—Ari asked, "Is all of that for me?"

"Yes." Ben held up the packet. "I talked to an old friend of mine today. He knows someone—a

guide down in Manaus—who is going to help you.''
Ben did not mention that Rafe Antonio would also
act as her bodyguard, because he knew Ari would
instantly rebel. Let his daughter think she was on her
own. He placed a color fax in her hands. ''This is a
photo of Rafe Antonio. He's a forest ranger near
Manaus. He's got a camp three hours east of there
on the Amazon River. I've hired him to help you
hunt for your orchids. You can stay at his camp,
which is near one of the Indian villages he takes care
of.''

Awed and stunned by her father's help, Ari held
the paper in her hands. The man in the photo wore
a short-sleeved khaki shirt with some kind of em-
blem on the sleeve. He was standing languidly on
what appeared to be a very old, beat-up houseboat.
She could see a wide, muddy river behind him. The
Amazon? She hoped so. He was so tall and athletic
looking as he rested his elbow on top of the wooden
pilot house. His face was square, his skin a golden
color, his hair short and jet-black. His eyes were
filled with laughter, and the wide smile showing his
even white teeth made her smile in turn. He looked
like an adventurer. Ari's heart began skipping wildly.
Rafe was terribly good-looking, in her opinion. Was
he married? Did he have a lot of kids? Ari thought
so. He looked married.

''He has a kind face, Father.''

Ben snorted. ''You're just like your mother, Ari,
thinking you can look at someone's face and know
him.''

"Sure you can." She saw her father frown in disapproval. Lately, she'd been getting awfully mouthy around him. Normally she kept such thoughts to herself. Ever since the desire to go to the Amazon had taken hold of her soul and heart, she couldn't keep the words, her true feelings, from spilling from her lips. Cringing inwardly, she saw the censure in his eyes.

"This man is to be trusted," Ben said with an effort. He didn't want Ari to know he was a mercenary in the employ of Perseus. Otherwise she would become suspicious. He had carefully extracted the info from the paperwork he was about to give her. "I'm leaving his résumé and curriculum vitae with you. You can read it on the flight down to Manaus. He's got a degree in biology. Where he works, there's plenty of orchids to keep you happy."

"Wonderful!" she gushed. "Oh, I'm so happy, Father. Thank you!"

"I don't approve of you going down there, Ari. Don't mistake what I'm doing. I'm very disappointed you aren't taking that job on Wall Street which I worked hard to get for you. You think life is easy. You think you can just traipse off on this airy-fairy dream of yours. You never took journalism in university. You need to do that if you want to write a book. And you don't have a degree in art. I don't know why you think you can create a book of orchids sketches with text and actually sell it." Raking his fingers through his hair, he pinned his daughter with a dark gaze. She hung her head and avoided his eyes, as always.

"I'm doing this for you because I know you'll do it anyway and I'd prefer you had my help. And dammit, I don't want to see you floundering around in a foreign country, in a strange city, trying to find someone who can help you hunt for orchids. Chances are you'd be robbed, killed or worse, kidnapped, and I'd get a call for a million-dollar ransom to get you back. No, Rafe Antonio is in place because I want you as safe as you can be on this jaunt of yours."

Pain filled Ari. "I—I understand, Father."

"How long do you think you'll be gone?" he demanded, barely keeping the anger out of his voice.

Looking from side to side, still afraid to meet his eyes, which Ari knew snapped with frustration, she said, "I don't really know. Mom said it would take at least three to six months to find enough orchids to fill a book. And then I'd need to go to New York to talk to publishers, get them to buy it."

Ben sat there helplessly. "Six months? You're going to be in Brazil for six months?"

"I don't really know, Father. It could be more or less. Mom figured it would take about thirty orchids per book. If I can find them sooner, I'll be back sooner."

"The sooner the better," Ben growled. He flung his hand toward the packet of information he'd tossed on the coffee table in front of them. "Read through the stuff. Antonio has a recent photo of you.

He'll know you on sight. He's going to meet you after you get out of Customs at the Manaus airport.''

Nodding contritely, Ari felt like crying. She was going on the adventure she and her mother had plotted and planned for months. During the last year of her mother's life, when she had been sick with leukemia, Ari had spent hours sitting on her bed, writing notes on the dream trip her mother yearned to take— but never would. That didn't stop her mother from imagining every day of it, however. And now Ari wanted to live that diary she'd filled with her mother's dreams. She wanted to fulfill them even if she couldn't draw or write very well. Ari was sure she'd never get the book sold, but she was going to try because it had meant so much to her mother, who had never had her dreams fulfilled. Ari was only sorry her father didn't understand why she had to go to the Amazon.

"I've got to leave," Ben said abruptly, and stood up. He rebuttoned his suit coat, smoothed his tie into place and gazed down at her. Ari seemed so fragile. Her skin looked so delicate that he could see the fine veins beneath her large, expressive blue eyes. In a robotlike motion, he reached out and briefly touched her sagging shoulder. "Have a good flight tomorrow, Ari. Call me when you get to Manaus?"

"Sure," she murmured. His touch was so brief, like a butterfly landing and leaving. Ari ached to have him pull her into his arms and embrace her in farewell. She quelled her own desire to fling her arms around him again. He seemed so embarrassed and uncomfortable when she did it. Crossing her arms against her chest instead, she kept her distance.

Ben pulled out a package from the inner pocket of his coat. "Here, a going away gift, Ari. Use it frequently."

Surprised, she took the gold-foil-wrapped gift, which sported a red ribbon. "Oh!" she gasped, and quickly sat down, tearing at the wrapping. When she opened up the long, rectangular box, she saw it held a phone. Looking up, a question on her face, she saw her father smile benignly.

"That's an Iridium phone—the latest technology available. It cost three thousand dollars. Use that to call me anytime. It hooks up to satellites directly. Cell phones don't work down in the jungle where you're going."

Touched, Ari gently put the gift on the couch. Against her better judgment, she threw her arms around her father. He was so tall! So strong and stalwart, when she felt none of those things about herself. Pressing her cheek against his chest, she sobbed, "Thank you, Father. Thank you…for everything…."

"Here, here," Ben growled as he gripped her upper arms and eased away. "Now don't go getting mushy on me, Ari. Buck up. And don't cry. I can't stand women crying."

Sniffing, Ari swallowed her tears of joy. "Okay, Father." She gave him a quick smile. "I'll call you when I land at Manaus."

"Yes," Ben said sternly, "you'd better." He

jabbed a finger toward the fax photo of the mercenary. ''And I want to know that you've hooked up
with Antonio. Do *not* leave the airport unless he's
there. Do you understand?''

Ari tried to look appropriately contrite as her father went through a three-minute list of what he did
and did not want her to do when she reached Manaus. Hands folded in front of her, unable to meet
his eyes, she simply bowed her head and listened, as
she always had. But her brain and heart were elsewhere while her father harangued her. Every time
she stole a look toward the coffee table and saw
Rafe's picture, her heart leaped like a wild gazelle.
Why? Ari was stymied. He looked to be in his late
twenties or early thirties. She was sure he was married. Well, it wouldn't hurt to enjoy how handsome
he was. She'd look, but not touch. Ari would never
think of liking a man who was married. She held
marriage sacred. Besides, she had been a wallflower,
with few dates coming her way in university. Most
men saw her as a weak-willed little thing incapable
of holding their interest.

Still, when her father finished his list and headed
toward the door, Ari brightened considerably.

As she quietly closed the door behind him, she
sighed with relief. She'd won. She'd taken her first
stand with her father and won. Her heart wouldn't
settle down, she was so excited. Walking back to the
couch, she eagerly sat down and looked through the
rest of the information on her guide. Ari was stunned
by his impeccable academic credentials. He'd gone

to Stanford Medical University and gotten a Ph.D. in biology! He was more than just a "forest ranger" as her father had said. Much more. Stanford's medical school was one of the top in the world for medical doctors and scientists. Obviously, Rafe was a scientist.

That thrilled her. He'd have a wonderful knowledge of her beloved orchids. Because he lived in the Amazon, he would know the species and varieties. As she quickly perused his résumé, she noticed he was single and twenty-nine years old. Single? She picked up the photo of him, stunned by this revelation. How could someone as drop-dead handsome as this man be *single?* That didn't make sense. Ari told herself he was probably divorced. Surely a man of his caliber, his looks and courage would have found his soul mate by now.

Rafe Antonio looked like a Spanish explorer from the sixteenth century, a world-conquering hero. The fax didn't give details of his facial features or the all-important eyes. Eyes, to Ari, were indeed the window to a person's soul which was probably why she was unable to meet most people's eyes—she felt excruciatingly vulnerable when she did. As if the person staring at her could look directly into her heart and soul. That kind of vulnerability was something Ari experienced twenty-four hours a day. She had no way to turn it off or protect herself.

But Ari didn't feel vulnerable now; she felt strong and alive. Unable to still the happiness that was palpably flowing through her like a river flowing over its banks in a springtime flood, she leaned back, closed her eyes and pressed Rafe's picture to her heart. Oh! How wonderful she felt! At last she was going to get to fulfill her mother's dream. How many books had they read on the Amazon? Ari remembered how her mother had read aloud to her as a seven-year-old. How she'd loved to hear her voice, for her mother knew how to make even the dullest book interesting, make the words come to life. Opening her eyes, Ari sobered a little. Yes, she was fulfilling a dream, but she feared she would never be able to draw the orchids well enough, or provide good text for the book.

"I have to try," she told herself fiercely, her words echoing around the room. Looking up, she gazed at a huge oil painting her mother had done of the Phalaenopsis, or moth, orchids. The petals really did look like moths' wings, she mused. The colors were rich and deep, from an elegant white orchid with pink luscious lips, to a pale yellow one and a vivid purple one. Their green, glossy oval leaves provided a fitting backdrop for the hanging spikes in the painting. Yes, there was no question that her mother was an exquisite artist. But Ari wasn't going to try and pretend that she was too. All she'd take with her to the Amazon was her sketchpad and her trusty set of colored pencils.

"Tomorrow, Ari, you'll be on your own for the first time...." And she was. She'd done everything her father wanted up until now. She'd gone to university. She'd lived in Georgetown and remained near his townhouse in the nearby suburb of Alexandria. Ari had been a faithful daughter to him by coming over to visit and making him dinner two or three nights a week. She'd been there for him as her mother might have been, if she'd lived. No, tomorrow was a brand-new chapter in her life and she knew it. Fear wound around her heart, yet Ari couldn't stop the excitement she felt. At last she was going to make her mother's dream come true...with the help of Rafe Antonio, a man who looked more like a Hollywood star than a forest ranger.

Chapter Three

Ari tried to balance her soft gold leather purse on her left shoulder, along with two pieces of luggage, as she hurried out of Customs at Manaus International Airport. She was late! When wasn't she? It was a terrible habit that seemed to dog her all her life. Voices of people anxious to meet their loved ones sounded around her as she stumbled along, most speaking Portuguese or Spanish. She heard very little English. People of all skin colors milled about or moved slowly through the narrow hallway that led into the receiving area.

Had she worn the right clothes? Though it was spring in North America, it was autumn here. Trundling along, Ari wished she were taller. At five foot six inches, she melted into the crowd of men, women

and children who moved good-naturedly but slug-
gishly forward, elbow-to-elbow. How would Senor
Antonio be able to find her? Anxiety rose in Ari.
What if he missed her? In her damp hand, she
clutched the fax with his photo. He was supposed to
be tall. That was good, at least.

Heart pounding with excitement and trepidation,
Ari tried to stand on tiptoe. In her sensible, dark
brown oxfords it was fairly easy to do. Colors were
everywhere. The people of South America looked
like colorful birds to her, their clothing bright and
patterned with elements from nature, such as flowers
and trees. The odors in the air ranged from spicy
perfumes to the tantalizing scents of food cooking
somewhere in the terminal ahead of her. The level
of excited expectation she felt keenly within the
crowd matched her own.

Where was Rafe Antonio? Anxiously, Ari peered
around. People were jammed ten deep along the cor-
doned-off area for passengers coming out of Customs. The faces of the awaiting families buoyed her
spirits. Happy cries drifted over the tumult and she
felt as if she were standing in a waterfall of languages, the air rent with the joyful calls of friends
and family to the arriving passengers. The glut of
people ground to a halt every time one of the awaiting families rushed forward to greet a loved one.

Ari found herself glued front and back to people
who had patiently stopped to allow others ahead of
them to greet one another. Everyone seemed highly
tolerant of the practice. Around her, people were

smiling. She relaxed somewhat. If this had been a North American airport, people would have pushed forward, elbowing their way out of the crowd. Not here. Ari marveled at the generosity of the people here and found her anxiety abating.

Standing on tiptoe again, she searched the masses of people. The crowd crept forward and she eagerly stepped along. It stopped and she pushed herself up on tiptoe once more. There! No... Well, maybe... At the very back of the crowd a man was standing. He was spectacularly handsome, his head and shoulders rising above nearly everyone around him. Rafe Antonio was supposed to be six foot five inches tall— a basketball player's height, in Ari's mind. Yes, this man was tall. Gorgeously handsome. Could that possibly be her guide for the coming months?

The man she was gazing at had tousled, wind-blown black hair, one dark lock dipping across his broad, golden forehead. He was wearing sunglasses which gave him the aura of a movie star. But the sweat-stained, short-sleeved khaki shirt he wore told her this was no movie star, but a man not afraid of hard work. The shirt was open, and dark hairs curled across his chest. Ari liked his square face and the strength of his jaw. His mouth was relaxed, the upper and lower lip the same thickness, with the hint of dimples surrounding them. He had a nice, kind mouth, Ari decided.

This man couldn't possibly be her guide. He was far too handsome, far too above the crowd; someone so confident in himself that Ari didn't dare think that he was, indeed, her mentor. Yet she liked the way he stood—relaxed, yet alert, his broad shoulders thrown back, his chin lifted regally. Oh, if only he was her guide! Ari giggled to herself. Her father would just die if he could get inside her head! Looking down at the picture in her hand and then standing on tiptoe once again, Ari wasn't sure. She hoped it was Rafe Antonio. He looked like he'd just come off the Amazon, sweaty and dirty, but that didn't deter her, nor did his unshaved face. It only made him look that much more of an adventurer, dangerous to her vulnerable emotional state.

Something niggled at Rafe as his gaze raked over the crowded airport terminal. He was a man used to picking up subtle sensations around him. Sometimes his life had depended upon such perturbations of warning. Yet this wasn't a danger sensation, but something else he couldn't put words to. The fact that he couldn't quite pinpoint it made him uncomfortable. A sizzle of anticipation wound through him. Every once in a while he'd catch sight of someone with blond hair bobbing up and down in the dense crowd. He couldn't quite catch sight of her, except for that cap of sunlight she wore. Was that Arianna Worthington? The rich socialite daughter of the secretary of the Navy? His instincts told him yes.

The thought made Rafe move closer, although he tried to tell himself he couldn't care less about this woman he had to baby-sit for Morgan. Oh, he'd tried to talk Morgan out of the assignment. Rafe didn't have time for rich young women who were out on a lark. His business was deadly serious and dangerous. He needed someone like Arianna right now like he needed a choke collar around his neck. Life in his region was unsettled and dangerous. Rafe didn't want to take time tending to the needs of a *norteamericana* who had never been in a jungle in her life.

He didn't try to elbow his way into the pack of awaiting people. Instead, he made his way behind the crowd, toward the exit. Thrusting his hands into the pockets of his strained and dirty khaki trousers, he smiled to himself. By meeting her at the airport filthy and unshaved, he hoped that she'd turn tail and run back to the States. He had been working on the houseboat engine, at the wharf, for six hours before having to come here. In the steamy, humid heat, he'd sweated plenty, adding to the dirt, grime and grease. He knew a lot about rich women, and Rafe figured that this one would find him absolutely repugnant. Hopefully, she would refuse to go anywhere with him because he looked like a filthy pig with no manners.

From this angle, Rafe could catch better glimpses of the golden-haired woman who stood in a mass of dark-haired people. Yes, he was sure it was her. His mouth drew into a hard line of impatience. Every time she thrust up on her toes, he caught sight of her for a few seconds. She was far more beautiful than the photo that had been faxed to him by Perseus yesterday. His heart pounded briefly every time he was able to catch a glimpse of her. Why did she have to be so beautiful? The only reason he'd grudgingly

agreed to meet this rich woman who wanted a jungle
adventure was because Morgan would write him a
check for one hundred thousand dollars, a donation
to his foundation to help the Juma, who were reeling
from losing half the people of their village in a bio-
terrorist attack. Rafe wanted the money to pay for
long-term medical needs for those who had survived,
and without such American dollars being pumped
into the village, many would suffer in great pain and
misery for many, many months to come. So Rafe
had capitulated; a socialite brat for three to six
months in exchange for money for one of the Indian
villages he was charged with helping and protecting.
Reluctantly, he studied her as she approached, trying
not to seem as interested as he really was. Arianna
Worthington wore a raspberry-colored cardigan
drawn around her shoulders, the sleeves tied in a
knot and hanging down the front. Her hair was gold
like the sun itself, thick and lying in a gentle frame
around her oval face, curling softly about her small
shoulders. But it was her eyes that intrigued him:
large, slightly tilted and the color of the sky he sometimes saw over the Amazon when the clouds decided
to part long enough to grant him a view. She looked
younger than twenty-five—somewhere between a
gawky teenage girl and a woman, he grimly decided
as he watched her try to balance the luggage she
carried. As the crowd thinned out, he started toward
her.

This was all he needed—an immature girl on his
hands. Even a rich socialite woman would be better

than this. Rafe, on the other hand, was mature beyond his years. His life-style, his responsibilities and the inherent dangers surrounding him, guaranteed that. His expectations fell further as he drew closer to her. She wasn't even self-confident, more like a frightened rabbit in unknown surroundings. Great. The word *baby-sitter* rang in his head and he felt anger.

In his world, he was a loner; he had accepted what he was a long time ago. His family was disdainful of his life as a backwoodsman. His father had disowned him because Rafe had refused to fill his parents' expectation that he would become a rich, powerful aristocrat in Brazil's government, as every son in the Antonio family had for the last two hundred years. Rafe was proud of what he did, but he did it alone. And not with something like this bedraggled-looking blond *norteamericana* hanging around his neck.

Rafe fought the protective feelings that rose in him as he looked at her. He noticed everyone looking at her, too. And why not? She was the only blonde in the airport. More than that, she was beautiful in an awkward though arresting way. The black, ankle-length cotton skirt decorated with splashes of pink, fuschia and plum flowers that she wore swung with each small step she took. In one hand, she clutched a piece of paper—probably his photo. In the other, a Panama straw hat, the type that could be rolled up and crushed into a suitcase.

Looking like a pack animal with her huge purse

and two attending black nylon bags, she labored under the weight. Seeing an opening in the crowd, Rafe slid smoothly through it in order to reach her. As he moved around several people, murmuring his apologies, he saw her catch sight of him.

Ari sucked in a huge gasp of air. It *was* him! The Hollywood star! Gulping, she froze. Rafe Antonio was like a tall, gorgeous god passing through the throngs of lesser beings. As he moved, he didn't disturb anyone. Instead, he had a boneless kind of grace that stopped her in her tracks. She stared in abject awe of him, as if he were a supernatural being.

Ari tried to stop her flights of fancy about this man, but it was impossible. As she stood there, weighted down like a mule, feeling disheveled and shamed because she felt so wretched compared to him, Ari could only watch him come closer, her heart pulsing powerfully.

As he glided effortlessly through the crowd, she watched as he lifted his hand and removed his sunglasses, placing them in the sweat-stained left pocket of his khaki shirt. When he looked up, she gasped again. His eyes were a cinnamon color—large, wide with intelligence and…something else. Aggravation? The sense of kindness about this man that had bowled Ari over at first seemed as if it was being replaced by the different emotions she saw in his narrowing eyes. She wasn't used to being so in tune with a man, and it shook her deeply to be able to tell so much of his emotions. To Ari, it was as if she were somehow invisibly connected to him, as if she were a seismograph registering every vibration she felt around him. It was a shocking sensation. And he was so incredibly handsome! She noticed a slight sheen of perspiration across his golden-colored skin and a smear of grease beneath the left side of his hard jawline. As his gaze met hers, Ari tried to pull away from his mesmerizing look. It was impossible. She felt drawn to him, to his soul, and the wildly exciting and powerful connection was overwhelming.

Dizzied and feeling terribly inept in his towering presence, Ari felt her purse sliding off her shoulder. Oh, no! It was a huge, oversize purse, one that she had packed with overnight accessories in case there was an emergency. As the heavy bag clunked to the floor, she tripped over it. With a cry, she went down on her hands and knees.

Rafe saw her fall, but he was too far away to catch her or break her tumble to the floor. The crowds parted quickly when people realized what had happened, so it was easy to sweep into the widening circle, slide his fingers around her arms and lift her back to her feet. She felt firm, yet soft beneath his hands. As he leaned over, he could smell the lingering scent of an exotic perfume. Perhaps a hint of jasmine. She was so close, so helpless in that moment.

"Oh…" Ari moaned as she looked up to see Rafe leaning over her, felt his strong hands grip her arms. She felt so embarrassed!

"Allow me, Señorita Worthington…." All of his

anger and trepidation ebbed away. She was helpless
and sweet, Rafe realized. Not a teenager, either. A
young woman. That was good.

His voice was deep, dark honey melting right
through to her wildly pounding heart. Ari felt his
hands slip around her upper arms to first steady her,
and then lift her as if she weighed nothing at all.
Humiliated by her fall, she tried not to look at the
people moving slowly around them. A number murmured to her in Portuguese and reached out and
gently patted her shoulder or arm, as if to help her.
Their kindness rattled Ari. She expected people to
ignore her and move around her, irritated and giving
her disdainful glances.

When Ari lifted her chin and looked up, up into
the warm brown eyes of the man who had rescued
her, she felt her knees going weak again. Instinctively, she grabbed at his forearms and felt the muscles there tighten. As she gripped him for support,
heat rolled up her neck and into her face. Now she
was blushing.

"I'm so sorry," she murmured apologetically.
"I—I'm such a klutz! I'm always stumbling and falling. What a mess I've made—again...."

Rafe gave her a tight smile. "*Señorita,* I'm Rafe
Antonio. Please, don't be apologizing. As you can
see, no one takes offense at what has happened. You
mustn't, either...." The look in her eyes was like
that of a wounded animal, or a child who had done
something terribly wrong. Why? Rafe wondered. Her
lovely oval face was flushed a deep pink color. Her

mouth… He quickly tore his attention from that
mouth, which reminded him of a beautiful rose opening in the morning sunlight. She was incredibly
beautiful in her own way, even if she was a spoiled,
rich *norteamericana* brat. He liked her broad forehead, her slightly angled blond eyebrows and those
flawless blue topaz eyes. Her nose was small, her
nostrils flared with chagrin. Though her chin was
weak, it completed the oval perfection of her face.
As she tried to get her balance, her thick, blond hair
moved like ripples on the surface of the Amazon
River he loved so much.

Ari couldn't stand Rafe's intense inspection and
she tore her gaze from his. Once she was upright,
she took a step away from him. He released one arm,
but carefully monitored his firm hold on the other.

"I'm okay…really, I am…." Then she realized
her lapse in manners. "I'm so sorry. I'm Arianna
Worthington, Mr. Antonio…." She thrust out her
hand. "Oh, and I speak some Spanish, if that's easier
for you."

Rafe took her proffered hand in his, leaned down
and placed a kiss upon the back of it. "Rafe Antonio
at your service, Señorita Worthington. And thank
you, but I prefer to use my English, as I don't often
get to speak it."

Ari was thrilled. His hand was huge compared to
hers and yet he held her fingers carefully, as if she
were delicate porcelain that might shatter with too
much pressure applied to it. As his strong mouth
grazed her flesh, a series of wild shocks leaped up

her arm. Her heart pounded violently in response. No one had ever kissed her hand before! She had to remember she was in a foreign country and that customs were different here. As Rafe raised his head, his brown eyes were hard and merciless looking. Was he unhappy with her? Most likely, Ari thought, her heart failing with pain. So was her father. She could do nothing to please him, either. Was Rafe like her father? The thought made her stomach knot.

"Oh...well, thank you, Senor Antonio...." She quickly pulled her hand away, her flesh tingling deliciously where his mouth had brushed it. Completely off balance due to his impeccable manners, his confidence and power as a man in charge, she felt like a blithering dolt in comparison.

"Call me Rafe," he murmured in response, picking up her luggage and handing her the purse. He didn't want to like her. She was artless. Or was it a ploy, like the one Justine, his ex-fiancée, had used on him? She'd been a careful manipulator of his heart and head, and had pretended a helplessness and innocence similar to what Arianna Worthington was now displaying. Was it an act? Was it real? Justine had played him like a harp, so much so that he had agreed to leave his jungle home, move to Manaus and continue his career as a paper pusher instead. One night Justine's mask had fallen off and he'd seen the real woman beneath—nothing like the one he'd fallen in love with. Rafe was wary of women since that experience. He knew they could play games, could be coy, manipulative and yes, pretend to be a bird with a broken wing. He gave Arianna a hard look. Was she a Justine in disguise? The thought was distasteful to him. He couldn't think of spending up to six months with such a woman.

Ari moved forward with Rafe leading the way. The crowd seemed to part miraculously for this man who stood head and shoulders above everyone else. Despite how he was dressed, Ari saw other people looking up at Rafe, admiring him, respecting his space. It was an unspoken thing and yet it was palpable and thrilling to her. What was it about him? His chin lifted at a proud angle, and his shoulders were so broad they took her breath away. The way he walked was wonderful to Ari. She wished she could have that same proud, aristocratic carriage.

"You can call me Ari," she said a little breathlessly as she hurried to catch up to him.

Rafe instantly reduced his stride. He realized that Ari was shorter and therefore had to take more steps to keep up with him. He looked down at her and found her face ablaze with a pink hue. She looked ill at ease. Twice she stumbled over her own feet and twice he reached out and gently took her arm to steady her.

"Thanks," Ari whispered, feeling shame. "I'm such a klutz...."

"There are a lot of people packed into a very small area," he told her as they eased away from the main part of the crowd and into the terminal itself. Outside the tall, vertical windows, he could see the humid white clouds above the city.

"I think I need a new pair of feet," she replied with an embarrassed laugh.

"Perhaps a new pair of shoes?" Rafe saw her avoid his eyes. Worse, he saw how she walked now that she was free of the confines of the crowd: her shoulders were slumped forward and her gaze flitted everywhere but to him. Her lack of eye contact worried him. She was acting like a beaten animal. Why? He had many questions. It bothered him how she was reacting to him, a man. Had her father beaten her? Rafe hoped not. As he watched her out of the corner of his eye he realized she was like a frightened child in a new place, her gaze darting here and there, her hands pressed to her heart as she hurried along, her body language telling him how terribly vulnerable she felt.

Halting near the doors of the terminal, Rafe put down the luggage and turned to her. Ari had been so busy looking around that she nearly ran into him. He put his hand out to steady her. What he wanted to do was simply pull her into the safety of his arms and hold her for just a moment. She looked like a scared little rabbit in a den of wolves. Rafe instantly rejected the protective feelings she conjured up. He was shocked by his reaction. This young woman was dissolving his normally iron-clad control over himself when it came to beautiful women.

"Sorry," Ari gushed as she jerked to a halt. Why hadn't she been watching where she was going? She felt so scattered, so out of control. Maybe her father had been right: going to a foreign country wasn't all it was cracked up to be. Overwhelmed, Ari absorbed the feeling of Rafe's hand on her upper arm. She felt bereft when he removed it.

"Let me tell you what we'll be doing, and perhaps that will make you feel a little more at ease," he murmured in a low tone. Her eyes widened considerably and Rafe saw the darkness in them—fear of the unknown, or a fear of him, perhaps. Unsure of her reactions, he purposely kept his voice low and his body language safe so that she wouldn't mistake any gesture as something threatening to her. He had hoped his attire would turn her off and she'd refuse to go anywhere with him, but such was not the case, he realized. She was sticking close to him, the world so overwhelming to her right now there was no way she was going to climb back on board a plane and leave.

"I'll get us a taxi outside the doors, here. And then we'll go to the wharf where my houseboat is tied up. Once we get on board, I'll take us downstream on the Amazon River, about three hours, and we'll pull into a side channel and that's where we'll stay. The channel leads to a Juma Indian village about a mile inland. That's where you'll be staying, Ari, and looking for your orchids to draw." His cool facade thawed a little. "I've never had an artist or a writer visit. I talked to Chief Aroka, the leader of the Juma village, and he's promised that he'll have some of his people who know the area help you search for orchids. They're looking forward to meeting you."

Grimacing, Ari held up her hands. It was almost too much for her to look into Rafe's eyes, but she had to. "Oh, dear...I don't know who told you I was an artist and writer, but I'm not! I've never gone to art school or taken journalism. I'm just trying to help my mother, who died, fulfill her dream of coming to the Amazon, to draw orchids and put them into book form. I'm sure I won't draw well enough for that to happen, but I want to try...."

In that instant, Rafe wanted to reach out, slide his fingers across the soft, smooth slope of her fiery cheeks and kiss her. The urge was powerful. Unbidden. Surprising. He had one hell of a time not staring at her mouth. Again it reminded him of a rose with fresh morning dew across it. He was sure she would taste sweet, soft and beguilingly beautiful. And then he remembered Justine had pulled a similar trick on him, playing innocent to get him to protect her, when in actuality she needed no protection whatsoever.

Shrugging, he said, "Who says you must have a degree in art or journalism to draw or write? Most of the people I know who have these talents have never experienced academia."

Heartened, Ari felt the warmth of his interest. The thawing look in his eyes was like sunlight shining on the frozen depths within her. His glinting gaze had such perception and she felt beautiful under it. For the first time in her life, Ari *wanted* to hold someone's gaze—his. He didn't make her feel as if he were stealing her soul, or some part of herself. No, his gaze was healing. It made her feel good about herself in a way she'd never felt before. So much was happening so quickly. It was too much for her to analyze right now.

"I just want to *try*," she told him in a husky voice riddled with tears. "For my mom. I don't know how much you know about me...."

"Very little," Rafe said, sorry that he didn't know more. A lot more. Was this an act? He wasn't sure if he were judging her because of his jaded past. Rafe found himself wanting to believe her, but he ruthlessly pushed that thought away.

Her hands fluttered about like bird wings as she continued. "Well...you'll get used to me. I'm just here to try and give Mom's dream reality. She was a wonderful artist. Her paintings were bought around the world by orchid fanciers and hobbyists." Looking down at her long fingers, Ari said, "I don't have one-tenth the talent she did...."

Rafe reached over and laid his hand lightly on her shoulder for a brief moment. He hadn't meant to touch her, but giving her solace felt like the right thing to do. "Where I come from, we say that when you paint or write with passion, from your heart, that's all that is necessary." He met and held her wide, tear-filled gaze.

He was irresistible! Choking back her tears, she whispered, "I like where you come from."

"Good." Still he held her unsure eyes. A part of him didn't want her to be coming back to camp with him. Yet her seemingly artless innocence was powerful medicine to his wounded heart. He was a loner,

Rafe reminded himself bluntly. Someone who had forsaken family dreams and expectations to blaze his own trail. No woman wanted him and the jungle he loved. There never would be such a woman as far as he was concerned. Justine had hated the jungle, the insects and the reptiles. She'd screeched over each little gnat that flew near her head. Shrugging away thoughts of Justine, he asked, "Are you ready to go, *señorita?*"

Ari nodded and gripped her purse. "Yes. Scared but ready, Rafe." His name rolled effortlessly off her tongue. She saw his mouth draw into a one-cornered smile. Again that sense of sunlight pierced through her and she felt unaccountably euphoric, as if lifted out of the morass of her own lingering anxiety and humiliation at stumbling to her hands and knees earlier. Rafe made her feel good. He was the first man to make her feel that. It was a wonderful, unexpected feeling, one that she absorbed like a thirsty sponge.

"Courage is taking a step at a time through your fear," he told her. Opening the door for her, he said, "Come, we must get a cab."

Ari was taken with his manners. He opened the cab door for her, too, and insisted she get in while he took care of the luggage. She felt overwhelmed by Rafe—his power, his charisma and good looks. When he slid into the seat next to her, he looked at her curiously, as if he were still trying to figure out what species of insect she was. His black brows had been drawn downward since he'd met her. With displeasure? Ari thought so and felt badly. She didn't want Rafe to feel like he was baby-sitting her. Perhaps she could show her mettle and tenacity at the camp and not be so much of a hindrance to him.

"Welcome to Manaus, Ari. It is a city that grew up from the rubber tree plantations earlier in this century. When the *norteamericano* companies created synthetic rubber, the boomtown here died. It has since resurrected itself mining gems, gold and other precious metals, plus a little tourism."

He barely fit into the dark green cab, but his large, masculine presence felt wonderful to her. Their arms and elbows touched in the cramped space, but Ari didn't mind. When he spoke in Portuguese to the driver, she smiled a little.

"How many languages do you know? You speak fluent English, Spanish and Portuguese, from what I can tell so far."

Rafe folded his large hands between his opened thighs as the cabby took off at high speed from the terminal. "I was raised in a family where knowing many languages was expected," he told her, meeting and holding her gaze. Now, instead of darkness in the depths of her eyes, he saw something else. Happiness? Perhaps a sense of safety now that she was away from the madding crowds of foreigners? He knew that being in a strange country made most people feel a little more vulnerable.

"Morgan Trayhern, your boss, sent me your résumé. It's impressive. I'm so thrilled you've got a Ph.D. in biology. And from Stanford. That is really something."

He nodded. "My knowledge of biology will help you a great deal in your quest for your orchids, Ari." As he said her name he realized how much he liked it. He liked saying it, and he was glad she wasn't a stickler for protocol, that she hadn't asked him to address her more formally, as they did in South America. She had surprised him in that regard. She wasn't some arrogant, rich brat with snobbish manners. Instead, she was simply herself. Or was she? Rafe knew time would yield that final answer.

"It must have been difficult to leave your family to come to the U.S. for your education," she said.

"Yes, I had to argue with my father to allow me to come to the States. I'm not sorry I did. I got an excellent education at Stanford."

Rafe was so easy to talk to, yet as Ari watched him, she realized that despite his relaxed state, he was keenly alert. She noticed that he watched everything in a casual, yet attentive sort of way. She felt an edginess within him, too. What was that all about? Was he disappointed with her? With the fact that she was such a klutz and a loser? That she was a woman he'd have to baby-sit? Determined to find out over time, Ari tried instead to focus on the joy bubbling in her heart as the cab sped rapidly onto a massive freeway. The tall buildings of Manaus were in the distance, the airport behind them. Ahead, she caught glimpses of a dark, tea-brown river. Was that the Amazon? Her pulse quickened. She was really *here.* She was on her mother's journey, the one they'd planned in such detail the last year she'd lived. Clasping her hands, Ari closed her eyes and took a deep breath, a wobbly smile tugging at the corners of her mouth.

Rafe felt Ari retreating within herself when she clasped her hands, sighed and closed her eyes. The flush in her cheeks had subsided and he noticed the porcelainlike quality to her skin. Blue veins were faintly visible beneath her eyes. She wore absolutely no makeup. It would be hopeless where they were going, anyway, with the rains and humidity. It made him feel good that she was so natural. Women who had to paint their faces into a mask were not their true selves, and Rafe admired Ari for her unspoken stand on the issue. Justine had insisted upon wearing makeup when she'd visited his camp. It had run and spotted, yet she was miserable without it. Why? Rafe would never understand why a woman couldn't be happy with her natural state, just as nature was with her bounty.

He saw that Ari wore simple gold hoops through her dainty earlobes. Around her neck was a fine gold chain holding an oval amethyst, to complement the skirt and sweater she wore. Everything about Ari spoke of delicacy.

Was she a hothouse flower? he mused. More than likely. Women with degrees from Georgetown University, who lived in Washington, D.C., were not equipped for jungle living. Would she be able to bear a life of hardship, without many amenities? Rafe doubted it. Justine had cried every morning because there wasn't electricity for her hair dryer. Would Ari see the jungle as her friend or her enemy? Probably an enemy, as his ex-fiancée had. Justine had been afraid to walk to the village with him, for fear of a snake biting her or some big bug whizzing by her head. Morgan had said Ari would be with him three to six months, depending upon how her sketches for the book came along. Rafe hoped it was a much shorter duration. Yet Ari intrigued him. So shy, yet with that childlike look of joy and anticipation written across her features. She was twenty-five, but she reminded him of a gawky fourteen-year-old who was just finding out who she was, just tapping into her femininity. He had no idea where his feelings and instincts about her came from; he'd lived so long on his instincts out in the jungle that he no longer tried to explain his sense of intuition about people. And he was rarely wrong about such perceptions because, over the years, his life had depended upon it. The one time he'd been wrong had been with Justine but she'd been a master of artful disguise and manipulation.

As the cab screeched to a halt some twenty minutes later, Ari looked out the window in anticipation. There was a huge river, at least a mile wide, spread out before her. Wobbly, poorly kept wooden docks jutted out from the raised, red dirt bank like dark dominos in the water. At one a huge white houseboat with black tires hanging off the sides was docked. That must be Rafe's. Before he could leave the cab and come around and open her door, she was out and walking quickly toward the riverbank. Hands clasped to her breasts, she looked around, absorbing all she saw.

The sky was clearing of soft white clouds that hung low over the dark green jungle along the river. She gasped when a flock of brightly colored scarlet macaws flew in a V formation right over her head toward the jungle in the distance.

Rafe came and stood next to her. "I see the goddess of the river has welcomed you to her breast."

Ari turned and looked up at him, a quizzical expression on her face. "River goddess?"

As the cabby came up with the luggage, Rafe told him to take it aboard the houseboat. Returning his attention to Ari, he saw the soft tendrils of her hair curling in the humidity. The maddening urge to tunnel his fingers through that thick, blond hair was almost his undoing. Instead, he cleared his throat and pointed to the quickly disappearing flight of parrots.

"The Juma believe that the mighty Amazon is a goddess. They pay her tribute by gifting her with bits of cornmeal or other food. The legend is that when she wants to leave her watery confines, she turns herself into a macaw to fly over her domain, to look after it, care for it and all her beings, including the two-leggeds. If Chief Aroka was here, he'd be shouting for joy that that squadron of macaws zoomed over your head at such a low altitude. He'd take that as a sign, a blessing, that the Amazon River goddess is welcoming you to her breast."

Sighing, Ari closed her eyes. "How wonderful...how absolutely beautiful! That must go in the

book. Oh, how I wish my mother could be here...."
She opened her eyes and held his dark gaze. "I know
she'd have sighed with joy over what you just told
me. These are the kinds of stories I want for my
book, Rafe! Please, just keep sharing these legends
and myths with me, will you? This is what I've come
down here for." She flung her arms open and
stepped forward. "The Amazon is *so* beautiful! So
wide. So grand! And how powerful she feels to me!"
Whirling around, the wind catching her skirt and lifting it to reveal her slender ankles, Ari laughed. It
was a laugh of joy, of surrender to the eternal beauty
of the Amazon jungle that now surrounded her. "I'm
in love! Truly in love! This all feels so wonderful to
me!"

Rafe stood there, enthralled by her spontaneity, by
the sunlight dancing in her wide, luminous eyes and
the soft parting of her lips into a smile that made his
heart pulse hard in his chest. The wind picked up
strands of her hair for a moment, as if she were being
caressed by the river goddess herself. He smiled tentatively. Surely this was no act on Ari's part.

"I see I don't have to worry about you fitting in
to our jungle. You're right at home, aren't you?"

Eagerly, Ari followed him to the rickety wooden
dock. "Yes, this *is* my home. I feel it here, in my
heart. I feel this energy, this sense of being alive for
the first time in my life, Rafe. I can't explain it, I
can only feel it." She gazed lovingly out across the
expanse of the mighty Amazon River, which looked
smooth and swirling, one moment a muddy color

like chocolate milk, the next a clear tea color. Ari could swear she felt the goddess of the river touching her heart, opening it; her chest expanded like sunlight to chase away the dark of the night she'd lived in all her life. She squelched the urge to throw her arms around Rafe's broad shoulders and hug him because she felt so incredibly happy. She didn't think he'd take kindly to such spontaneity.

When they reached the plank that led from the dock to his houseboat, he put out his hand to her. "Allow me?"

Automatically, Ari gave him her hand. There was no hesitation on her part, just a sense of that trust he inspired in her. As his strong, callused fingers closed around hers, she breathed in deeply. "I feel like I'm about to board this boat and step into another world!"

Rafe led her up the plank and onto the worn deck of the houseboat. "You're more right than you know, Ari." He pointed to the cabin. "Down there are your living quarters. The cabby put the luggage there. If you want to change into something more comfortable for our trip downstream, why don't you? I'm going to cast off the lines and get underway." When she saw the disheveled living conditions, he was sure she'd be disappointed. He wondered if she'd wail and cry like Justine had when he'd picked her up at this very dock to take her back to his camp.

Ari nodded. "Do you mind if I watch you cast off?"

"No, not at all." He grinned a little. She was like a wide-eyed child who had never seen a boat before.

"So much for our Manaus visit," he told her as he crossed the plank.

Stymied, Ari stood there and felt the gentle rocking of the boat beneath her feet. "What do you mean, your 'Manaus visit'?"

Untying the stern, Rafe threw the hemp rope onto the deck. Then he hurried forward and unknotted the bow line. "I come to Manaus in an official capacity for the city, for whom I work, as few times a year as I can get away with." He leaped onto the boat, picked up the boarding plank, placed it on the deck and tied it down. "Most of the time I'm in the jungle, my real home. Coming to the city is painful to me. I don't like the sounds, the noise or the congestion." As he rose to his full height, he held her gaze. She was still standing there, her hands clasped to her breast. There was something innocent and pure about Ari that he'd seen only in children—never in a woman. And she was certainly a woman.

"And you prefer your jungle home?"

He climbed the ladder to the cockpit, situated on top of the galley and living quarters and protected on three sides by wood and glass panels. "How do you say it? I'm a country boy at heart? That is *norteamericano* slang for where my spirit lives." He took a key out of his pocket and inserted it into the console. With one twist of the key the motor began to growl and white water began to churn at the stern.

Suddenly, Ari wanted to join him in the cockpit.

But she realized Rafe was right: she had to get out of her skirt. If she tried to climb that ladder, she'd trip and hurt herself. She'd shown him her awkward side already and she wasn't about to do it again.

"Hey, wait just a minute? Let me change. I want to join you and see how you get out of here."

Rafe nodded as he watched her bolt across the deck and hurry down the wooden steps. "Sure," he called. "Take your time. We're in no hurry." Stunned that she obviously relished being on the boat and looked forward to seeing more of the river and jungle, he shook his head. Was he loco? Or was she? Ari's reaction to everything seemed genuine. Her enthusiasm was infectious, and he found himself feeling a tad better about her being at his camp.

As he gazed across his beloved river at the dark green jungle on the other side, Rafe sighed deeply. He felt smitten, a little giddy with joy. All because of Ari. What a wild and natural woman she appeared to be. Was she really? That would be too much to hope for. He wasn't sure she really even knew herself. She was more spontaneous child than conservative adult. He grinned sourly. He hadn't known what to expect with Ari. Since she was the daughter of a powerful man in the U.S., he'd thought she'd be confident, arrogant and very socially conscious. Well, scratch his assumptions; Ari was none of those things.

As he looked around, the gentle movement of the boat comforting him like a welcoming lover, Rafe smiled again. Life was full of surprises. He didn't know what he'd done to deserve the gift of Ari Worthington, but one thing was for sure, he was going to give the river goddess her due for such an incredible surprise. *If* Ari was a gift and not a lie wrapped up in a beautiful package. Life had never looked brighter—or more hopeful to him on one hand. On the other, he was wary of Ari and her reasons for being here. In his business, he was alone most of the time. Women of his station would refuse to have a relationship with him—much less think of marriage—because he was never in Manaus. He lived and worked in the jungle—where his heart was, where his soul thrived.

Glancing below, Rafe placed his hand lovingly on the wooden wheel and waited patiently for Ari. She was worth waiting for because he would now see the Amazon through her eyes. The eyes of a child-woman who was enthralled with the beauty of this incredible place on the Equator, a beauty few people knew of. Yes, life was more hopeful, more tempting, than he could ever recall. Then again, Justine had acted just as enthralled about the journey to his camp, too. In due time, Rafe would begin to see the real Arianna Worthington. One way or another.

Chapter Four

Breathless with anticipation, Ari hurried up the teakwood steps. She noted that they were sadly in need of sanding and revarnishing. The houseboat was very old, well worn and lived in, she realized, now that she'd had a chance to see the living quarters. Rafe was obviously neat and clean, despite his disheveled appearance at the airport, though everything was cramped down below. There was a sofa that doubled as a bed. The shower was tiny. The galley kitchen was spick-and-span, but small. Still, it would be her home away from home for the next three to six months. That made her feel giddy. She had been expecting to rough it, but the houseboat was a wonderful surprise.

Quickly trying to smooth her hair into place because she'd mussed it while haphazardly shrugging into a crimson tank top and jeans, she found herself more than eager to be with Rafe. In her hand, she had her faithful leather-bound journal and a pen—just in case he had another story to tell her.

Rafe heard Ari clambering noisily up the stairs. Against his better judgement, he grinned a little as she emerged. Her hair looked flyaway, an unruly golden mop around her face and shoulders. Still, it did nothing but make her look more beautiful in his eyes. She wore a brilliant red tank top that nearly matched the flush on her cheeks. He saw with pleasure that she wasn't going to be a fashion dresser. That was a surprise to him. Instead, she wore a pair of soft, serviceable blue jeans that were loose enough that she could comfortably hike in them. He liked the dark brown leather belt with the sterling silver heart clasp that she wore. Yes, he suspected grudgingly, Ari was all heart, all passion. His emotions reeled from this possibility. Rafe kept trying to reject her because she came from a rich, powerful family, as Justine had. And as he had.

"Whew! That was the fastest change I've ever done," she confided with a glowing smile as she stood nervously outside the cockpit.

Rafe pointed to the other chair, which was bolted to the deck next to him. "Come on in. Sit down."

"Thanks," Ari whispered, barely able to meet the curious warmth burning in his eyes. Her heart skittered as her left elbow brushed against his dark, hairy arm. Settling herself in the well-worn wooden chair, she looked around. "I'm so excited! This is a dream come true, Rafe. You have no idea...."

"I'm getting there," he murmured dryly, draping his fingers across the twin throttles on the console. When he reversed the engines, the houseboat began to slowly back away from the dirt bank and the rickety old dock.

Ari held the large journal in her lap, gripping it firmly. She liked the quiet way Rafe nudged the houseboat out into the river. The gentle floating motion of the craft was soothing to her fractured nerves. "This feels so nice," Ari said, then sighed as she gazed at the incredible expanse before them. "The rocking of the boat reminds me of the times my mother would hold and rock me when I was feeling bad, or when I was sick."

Rafe pointed the bow of the boat downstream, toward where two major rivers joined to create the Amazon. No matter how hard he tried to focus on piloting and keep Ari far from his thoughts, it was impossible. How could she reach inside him so quickly and touch his heart?

"You said it was a dream come true," Rafe said, glancing past her head as he spotted a huge log bobbing just below the surface of the water. It was coming directly at them and he swung the wheel to the left to avoid it. If one of those big logs hit the houseboat, it would punch a hole in the hull and they would sink very quickly. The area they were crossing was where the rivers combined, the current tricky and surprising. Logs and debris could come from any direction at this point of the journey.

"Yes. How much did my father tell you about me?"

Rafe kept his gaze on the log. The Amazon current was deceptive. The river was wide and deep. It looked fairly calm on the surface, but that was an illusion. The log was traveling with the current, at a good six or seven miles per hour. "Actually, I received information on you through Morgan Trayhern at Perseus. He's a close friend of your father's." Rafe didn't want Ari to know he worked for Morgan and added, "Morgan is a friend of mine, also." It wasn't a lie—just not the whole truth. He angled the houseboat a little more to give the log a wide berth. "He sent me your curriculum vitae, that was all."

"I see...." Ari watched the dark, waterlogged tree, which was at least a hundred feet long and more than three feet in diameter, slide on by them. From the looks of things everything was big down here in the Amazon. And then she laughed to herself. Look at Rafe; he was a huge man! Tall like the proud and mighty trees she saw growing on the distant shore. Not many men stood six foot five. He carried it well. In her eyes and heart, he looked like a warrior from another era. A knight came to mind. Yes, he would definitely be at ease in the age of chivalry. He was such a gentleman in a time when the practice of opening doors for women and carrying their luggage was practically nonexistent, at least in the U.S.

"Tell me about your mother's dream," he urged,

steering the houseboat toward where the rivers merged. Inwardly, Rafe chastised himself for his nosiness. But Ari invited such close inspection whether he wanted to acknowledge it or not. All around them, currents swirled in clockwise and counterclockwise currents as the two rivers joined one another. It was always a little chaotic in this stretch, but Rafe was used to traversing the currents with his trusty, sturdy houseboat.

Ari told him about her youth. When she got to the part about Janis dying, her voice ebbed to a painful whisper. "Janis was several years older than me. My big sister. She was such a daredevil. She loved to ride horses. My parents gave her a horse when she was five. And by nine years old, she was entering jumping competitions in her age group—and winning!" Ari smiled sadly as she felt his gaze settle on her. When she looked over, she met and held his eyes for a moment. Quickly looking away, she said, "Janis took a dare from a boy at the stable where her horse was boarded. He dared her to jump a four-foot stone wall." Flailing her hands helplessly, Ari continued, "Janis had never jumped four feet with Rosebud, her horse. But she loved challenges and she tried to make the jump. Rosebud balked at the last moment, throwing her into the wall." Closing her eyes, Ari whispered, "Janis died of a broken neck on the spot. I learned about it later that day. I was so shocked."

Rafe saw her knitting her hands nervously in her lap atop the leather-bound journal. "That must have been very hard on you. Did you have any other siblings?''

''Yes, Kirk. He's the oldest. He was fourteen at the time Janis died. Everyone was devastated, as you can imagine.''

''Especially you?'' Rafe inquired gently. He saw the terrible loneliness and grief etched in her sky-blue eyes. Wanting to reach out and cup her cheek, let her know that someone else felt the pain of her loss, Rafe quickly squelched the impulse. Being around Ari was disconcerting. His protective instincts were on full alert. But the last thing he wanted to do was get involved with any woman again. Justine had wounded him too deeply for him to allow his feelings to resurface. Normally he was in tight control of himself. With Ari, he found himself aching to touch her, just to give her solace, or to share a joyful moment with her. And yet she was so painfully shy and timid. He was beginning to understand that losing her big sister as a vulnerable eight year old had taken a lot of vitality out of her.

''We were close. Really close,'' she admitted hollowly. ''After that…well, my mother fell ill. Really ill. About six months after Janis was buried, she fainted. They took her to the emergency room at the closest hospital. The doctors said she had a particularly aggressive form of leukemia. They didn't give her more than a year to live, even with chemotherapy treatments.''

Rafe stared at her, his jaw dropping momentarily. He quickly hid his reaction from Ari. Her eyes were huge and sad now. "That's a tragedy," he murmured, meaning it. To lose a parent was particularly devastating. Rafe knew from personal experience.

"She died a year later, to the day," Ari said, gazing around at the muddy expanse of the Amazon as they began to drift closer to the right bank. Forcing a smile she didn't feel, Ari looked up at Rafe. His black brows were drawn down and she was shocked to see anguish, for just a second, in his eyes. Her father never showed his grief over her mother's passing. She had never seen him cry. He had stood at the funeral tall, strong and unmoving. It was she, Ari, who had sobbed for the two stoic males in her family. She'd cried for weeks after that, without end. To realize that Rafe was showing his feelings was a shock to her.

Mesmerized by that discovery, Ari simply stared up at him. So men could feel and emote. It was a wonderful discovery to her. The boys at Georgetown University were nothing like this man who stood so tall and knightly before her. But then, Ari reminded herself, Rafe was not a boy. Clearly, he was a mature man, even emotionally. That thrilled her. Scared her. She had no idea how to react to a man who could share his feelings with her so openly. They barely knew one another, yet he was unveiling his vulnerability to her. Trust...he trusted her. The concept was euphoric. Frightening.

Rafe felt her inspection of him. He purposely didn't turn to meet her eyes, though. Let her look him over real good. He knew to treat her just as he did the wild animals he encountered. In the forest, when he came upon a herd of wild pigs, they wouldn't flee unless he looked them squarely in the eyes. Instead, he'd halt, remain motionless and allow them to gauge him with their senses. When he did that, they would remain and continue digging for roots, or they'd amble off without squealing in fear. Ari was just like a wild animal in some respects, he was discovering. Still, her nervousness told him that she didn't know what she was getting into in spending months in the Amazon.

"Losing two of the most important people in your life when you were eight had to be a special hell." He shook his head, his hands tightening momentarily on the aged wooden wheel he stood over. If he didn't grip hard, he was going to reach out and gently curve his hand across the top of her wispy golden hair, to soothe the grief he heard in her soft voice. The impulse alarmed Rafe. How could this waif inspire such a powerful feeling in him so suddenly?

"It's been hard," Ari admitted. Patting the journal on her lap, she said, "Mom asked both of us to come to her bedroom every day. Kirk didn't want to. I think he was afraid and couldn't stand the thought of losing her, or seeing her slip away from us, month after month."

"But you did?"

"Yes. And you know what my parents did? It was the most wonderful gift of all. They took me out of school for that last year of my mom's life. She tutored me at home, on her bed. On good days, if she felt like it, we'd be in the living room and she'd sit on the couch. On bad days, she'd stay in bed and I'd sit cross-legged on the quilt, just listening to her, or reading to her from one of her favorite books.''

Satisfaction soared through him. ''That was a beautiful parting gift.'' Try as he might, Rafe could no longer see Ari as rich, spoiled and inexperienced, though he struggled to hold that view of her. He had to.

''It was my father's idea.''

''He saw how close you were to your mother and probably realized the loss of Janis had so devastated you that you needed that time with her. Time to help heal yourself and say your goodbye to your mother.''

Shrugging, Ari said, ''I don't know. My father is like a fortress, Rafe. He doesn't cry. He doesn't show emotion, except for his anger and disgust over my bad decisions. That's the only way I've ever seen him.'' She almost added, *I wish he was more like you,* but bit her lower lip instead. Sometimes she gushed too spontaneously. Her father often accused her of hoof-in-mouth disease.

''Men can be stoic,'' Rafe agreed. He pointed ahead. ''Look, another flight of macaws. This has to be your day.''

Excitedly, Ari slipped off the chair and walked outside the cockpit on the upper deck. The humid air swirled around her, embraced her, and it felt wonderful to her. In her imagination, it felt like a loving embrace. The river smelled clean, despite the odor of mud that lifted to her nostrils. There were other faint fragrances and she wondered if they were from orchids hiding in the trees on shore. Lifting her chin, she looked in the direction Rafe had pointed.

Eight yellow-and-blue parrots were flying swiftly, barely twenty feet above the water's dark chocolate surface, directly toward them. They flew with short, stubby wings, in a caliper formation. To her delight, they came within ten feet of the bow of the houseboat. "Oh! I wish I had my camera!" Their bright turquoise feathers and stunning sun-gold plumage coupled with the white flesh around their eyes and powerful beaks made her gasp with delight. "They are so beautiful!" She threw her hands skyward in joy.

Rafe wished he'd had a camera, too—to take a photo of her innocence and spontaneity. As she turned, a whimsical look on her features, he laughed deeply in surprise and wonder. When he did, he saw redness stain Ari's cheeks. She instantly changed. Instead of holding her head up and her shoulders back, she shrank into her old self—head down, shoulders rounded, eyes downcast on the deck of the boat. Cursing himself, Rafe realized she'd interpreted his laughter as poking fun at her spontaneity. As she walked slowly back to the cockpit and quietly resumed her chair, he spoke.

"I wasn't laughing *at* you, Ari. You thought I was making fun of you, didn't you?"

Stunned, she jerked her head up and met his dark, stormy-looking eyes. "Well, uh, yes…yes, I did. My father says I'm too spontaneous—that I'm supposed to be twenty-five years old, not eight years old."

Suddenly, Rafe didn't give a damn about his own distrust of women. He reached out and gently rested his hand upon her slumped shoulder. "Listen to me, my wild nature child, you should *do* what you just did out there on the deck when those parrots flew by. Do it often." He saw her eyes widen with shock. Moving his fingers in a grazing motion across her shoulder, he added, "Wait until you meet the Juma Indians. You'll feel right at home. They are adults and yet they hold the awe of children in their hearts and heads, too. You are exactly like them, so let that side of you strut its stuff." He grinned a little and forced himself to stop touching her. Her skin beneath the cotton tank top felt deliciously smooth and firm. "Is that a deal? Will you promise me to jump up and down? Throw your hands to the sky? Yelp? Yell? Be a wild woman?"

Her flesh tingled hotly where he'd touched her. There was such controlled strength in Rafe's touch. Ari couldn't have torn her gaze from his dark, incisive one if she'd wanted to. Something warm and strong in his deep voice moved through her like the low growl of a jaguar to its mate. Her heart swelled. Her pulse skittered. "Well, sure… I thought I'd embarrassed you or something. Father always gets nervous and uncomfortable if I do things like that."

"Thank goodness," Rafe said dryly, "I'm *not* your father. So you just go on and be the child of Mother Earth. Okay?"

Smiling tentatively, Ari felt herself arch inwardly as she heard his deep, rolling laugh. "Okay."

"The Juma have a saying," Rafe continued as he angled the boat about a hundred feet off the reddish bank of the river where the current was less feisty. "They say that to really live, to touch the fire and passion of your soul, you must have the heart and head of a child."

Ari opened the journal and quickly scribbled down his words verbatim. "That's wonderful. Thank you."

"You can live your life as an adult. You can behave in a mature manner when it's demanded," Rafe said conversationally, "but believe me, every time I get a chance to revert back to being a big kid, I do it. I play grown-up when I have to. Otherwise—" he gave her a wicked, teasing look "—I'm really a ten-year-old boy inside this man-size frame of mine."

Laughter bubbled up from Ari's chest and into her throat. She absorbed the deviltry and teasing in his cinnamon-colored eyes. The smile he shared with her was absolutely devastating and catalytic to her. Did Rafe realize that when he rewarded her with that brilliant smile, showed her those even white teeth, she felt like swooning like a woman from Victorian times? Ari thought not. He seemed to be unaware of his powerful effect upon her.

"And so the man I saw back at the airport, that Hollywood Hunk, is a facade? Just a mask?"

Raising his brows, Rafe said, "Hollywood Hunk?

Where did *that* come from?'' And he barely resisted laughing with her.

Heat flamed into Ari's cheeks, though he took her teasing gracefully and without rancor. Emboldened, she said, ''Well, I certainly wasn't expecting to see this man who stood head and shoulders above the crowd, like a knight out of old England, waiting to meet me. You looked like a Hollywood star to me when I first saw you. With those dark glasses.'' Ari looked away. ''I have such a runaway imagination!''

''What else did you think?'' he asked. ''I like the way you see me. Who wouldn't?''

Waving her hands nervously, Ari muttered, ''Who wouldn't? No one ever reminded me of a movie star until I saw you. It's this sense of power—something—around you....''

''Charisma?''

''Yes, that's it! You have an almost magnetic kind of charisma. When I was searching the terminal for you, I instinctively felt pulled to look in a certain direction, and there you were!''

''Your Hollywood Hunk?''

Giggling, Ari met his smiling eyes. ''That's what I thought—guilty as charged. Just blame my flights of fancy. My mother always said I was very creative, and she encouraged me to look at things, at people, in that way. Some people remind me of a steel-and-glass building. Others of gnarled old oaks.''

''Pwhew, I got off lucky. I'm the Hollywood Hunk.''

Her laughter grew until it floated around her musically. Wiping the tears from her eyes, she muttered, "I can't recall laughing so much, so often."

He touched his chest with his hand. "I'll accept the blame." Did Ari realize how incredibly beautiful she was when she laughed? Did she know that her wide, sky blue eyes shined with gold highlights, as if the sun itself had taken up residence within her? Her mouth was soft, full and delicious looking when she laughed, so alluring, tempting him to kiss her and absorb that smile through his own lips and into himself. It was a perfectly selfish desire. One that gnawed insistently at him. He studied her as the breeze ruffled her golden hair and the afternoon sunlight glinted through the clouds to touch her. For a moment, her face was framed in sparkling sunlight and she looked more angelic than earthbound. And then, just as quickly, the sun was hidden once again by the ever-present, low-hanging cumulus clouds. For once in his life Rafe was at a loss of words.

"How knightly of you," Ari teased back as she pressed her hand to her heart, her chest aching with spent laughter. She watched as Rafe gave her a suave smile. Getting to know him was like opening up a treasure chest of gold, emeralds, sapphires and diamonds; he was an endless bounty of gifts to her heart and wounded soul.

"Ah, the knight part." He gave her a courtly bow. "Tell me more, milady, of how you see me in this guise?"

"You're such an egotist!"

"Me? No. You're the one calling me knightly. I

just want to hear more of how you see me," he cajoled, and met her smiling eyes. Rafe knew he shouldn't be engaging her on a personal level like this. He wanted to think of her as rich, spoiled and pampered. He didn't want to get close to her.

"After I got over thinking you were a movie star, and as you drew closer, so tall and seemingly untouched by the crowd around you, in my imagination I saw you as a knight. A knight from old England who went around saving the weak and protecting the underdogs from harm. There was this wonderful sense of protectiveness that I felt...still feel...around you, Rafe." Nervously, Ari opened her hands, unsure of how far to go with her creative musing. At this point, her father would have been giving her a thundercloud look for such ramblings. Risking everything because Ari remembered that Rafe liked her spontaneity, she blurted, "I imagined you as Sir Galahad who sought the Holy Grail. Your face has deep, cutting lines in it—slashes around your mouth, wrinkles on your brow. That tells me you've been through a lot, but that even if you have been wounded by life's trials, you still keep your dream of finding the Grail. No matter what."

Rafe gave her a look of praise. "Do you read minds?"

"What? Me?" Ari laughed uncomfortably. "No. Why?"

"Because," he murmured, impressed, "you hit the proverbial nail on the head, to borrow a *norteamericano* saying." His hands steadied on the boat as the shore grew closer. They were now drifting about fifty feet from the dry, sandy bank.

"How?"

"Well," Rafe continued with a sigh, "it's my turn to share a little of my family history with you. My father owns, roughly, twenty-five banks in Brazil. I come from a very rich, powerful and influential family. I was the firstborn son, and naturally, my father expected me to get an MBA and learn the banking business from him and eventually, when he retired, take over his empire."

Ari stared up at him. Right now, she felt Rafe's sadness. It was expressed in the line of his mouth, now compressed, and in the way his deep voice was serrated with old, unresolved grief. "You didn't do that, though? You went to Stanford and got a Ph.D. in biology instead."

"I defied my father from the time I was old enough to know what the word *no* meant," he said.

Laughing politely, Ari said, "Kirk, my brother, was a lot like that, too, growing up."

"Maybe it's a boy thing?" Rafe mused, enjoying talking with her. There was a surprisingly deep maturity and understanding he hadn't thought possible in Ari. Realizing she was old beyond her years made him hungry to converse with her.

"I don't know about that. I wanted to say no, but when I watched Kirk and Janis get it from my father, I knew better."

"Ah, yes, the knock-down, drag-out fights...I know them well."

"You didn't turn out to be like your father at all?"

"No, I am like my mother. She is a medical doctor and a fine scientist. Her love is virology and micro-biology. It was she who taught me the love of the jungle surrounding Manaus. My father disapproved of her taking me with her on her field trips to find new viruses in the rain forest. I fell in love with the trees, with the land, the animals…the people. From the time I was eight years old, I knew what I wanted to be—a backwoodsman."

"A forest ranger?"

"One and the same, yes."

"Did your father finally understand? Did he bless your decision to do what you're doing now?"

Brows knitting, Rafe looked down at his long, large-knuckled hands. There were so many scars on them, white and pink ones, older and newer ones. "No…" he admitted slowly, pleased at Ari's under-standing of him. "When I told him I was going to Stanford—that I wouldn't be following in his foot-steps—he disowned me."

"No!" Ari gasped. She nearly came out of the chair, then stopped herself, staring at his rock-hard profile and seeing the anguish clearly evident in his face. "Surely he eventually forgave and forgot?"

Shaking his head, Rafe gave her a rueful glance. "No, not to this day. My mother sent me money to go to Stanford. I held a lot of odd jobs to make the rest of my tuition. She couldn't always send me money because if my father had ever found out, all hell would have broken loose, for sure. He never understood my love of the people who live in the basin.'' He made a wide, sweeping gesture toward the bank, where thousands of trees, palms and ferns lined the river like an unbroken corridor in different hues of green, ranging from evergreen and olive to chartreuse.

"How terribly sad.'' Ari felt hot tears steal into her eyes. She saw him give her a sharpened look. "Sorry, I cry at the drop of a hat. My father *hates* to see me cry.''

Leaning over, Rafe slid his fingers along the clean line of her jaw. Her eyes flared with shock, surprise and something else…pleasure, perhaps. But that was not why he'd followed his heart and touched her. "The Jaguar Clan has a saying, my wild woman. That if we cannot shed tears from our heart for those who suffer, then we are made of stone.'' Grazing her flaming cheek, his fingers tangled briefly in the gold of her hair along her temple. If he didn't stop, he'd kiss her. Shocked, Rafe pulled away and moved uncomfortably back to the wheel. Where had the words *wild woman* come from? He'd spoken them like an endearment, something intimate and private that he wanted to share only with her.

Without thinking, Ari put her hand to her cheek where he'd touched her like a butterfly grazing a sweet, honey-filled flower. The tenderness in Rafe's normally hard expression shook her to her soul. This man…this person who seemed to know the very center of her heart, had touched her as she'd never been touched before. No one had ever sent burning tingles of pleasure across her sensitized flesh as he had. No one had held her heart with such tenderness. Blinking back tears, Ari could only sit there and absorb the moment. She couldn't think, could only feel. Her heart throbbed like a rainbow burning high in the blue sky above them. Surely this was how a rainbow felt, she thought as she moved her fingers lingeringly across where her heart lay, open and vulnerable.

Gathering her courage, Ari whispered, "In my eyes—my heart—you're a knight in shining armor. Look how you care for and protect the Indians in the territory you have responsibility for. The people must love you for your dedication to them. I'm so sorry your father can't realize your dream, your vision. I hope someday he will."

Quirking his mouth, Rafe said, "Not a chance, Ari. He's set in stone. The stone that the Jaguar Clan refers to. He's all head. He's buried his heart and feelings a long time ago. I'm afraid he's got an ego the size of São Paulo, and São Paulo has fourteen million people in it."

"But," she said, opening her hands, "how do you stay in touch with your family, then?"

"I have my ways." He smiled a little savagely. "My two younger sisters and brothers live in Manaus beneath his shadow, doing what he wants them to do with their lives. My mother and I have a secret code so that when I call her on a certain phone line, she knows it's me. I usually meet her at my home, which sits on the outskirts of Manaus."

"At least you get to see them." Still, Ari saw the

damage that his father had done to him. Saw the agony in his eyes and the way he stood rigidly at the wheel. Her heart ached for him. "I didn't know you had a house in the city. I thought you lived here," she said, gesturing to the houseboat.

"I do live out of this," he told her. "When I'm not tracking illegal miners, drug runners or drug lords on the land, I use a small aluminum skiff with a motor to move around in the back channels of the Amazon. I keep the houseboat tied up in a channel near the Juma village. They watch over it when I'm away on a mission."

"Then the house in Manaus is..."

He smiled. "I work for the State, so I have to have residency there. About twice a year I go in and report on what's happening in my territory, create a budget and tell the board how the money will be spent for the coming year. That kind of thing. It usually takes a week to do that."

"And that's when you see your family?"

"Yes."

She heard the satisfaction in his voice. "In my eyes, you're still a knight," she said, and gave him a small smile.

Rafe nodded. "A tarnished knight banished from his land and from his family. Not exactly storybook material, am I? More of a disappointment."

Frowning, Ari shook her head. "You have problems with your father just like I do." She rested her elbows on the journal and planted her chin in her cupped hands. "We're lucky to have the moms we did—or do."

"My mother's a pearl," Rafe said. "My father doesn't deserve her, but for whatever reasons, she hasn't walked out and left him."

"Mmm, I understand. Maybe our fathers should get together?"

"From the sounds of it, World War III would start." Rafe snorted and then gave her a wry smile. He looked down at his watch. "Well, in another hour we'll be at the village…and your new home." How would she react? Rafe was curious.

Heartened, Ari smiled and sat up straight. "I can hardly wait to see it! I would read books to my mother about the Amazon Basin, about all the trees, plants and beautiful, undiscovered orchids that grew there."

"Does what you read stack up against the real thing?" he asked, as he gestured to the triple canopy jungle to the right of them.

"Yes. A thousand times over!" Ari clapped her hands. "Even from here I can see what I think are red and pink bromeliads peeking out here and there. Sometimes I wonder if it's my overactive imagination, or just tricks of shadows and light as the sun runs and hides behind the clouds."

"You're seeing right," Rafe replied, congratulating her. "You've got a keen eye. A trained one, as a matter of fact." He pointed to a twisted and gnarled rubber tree that grew near the edge of the jungle. "See that? The tree with the grayish looking bark?"

"Yes. A rubber tree, right?"

He grinned. "Right. Look up toward the top of it, on that one branch that looks like an arm bent backward. See those long, spiky leaves shooting out from the joint area?"

Excitedly, Ari followed his direction. "Yes, I see it."

"That's a bromeliad. A red one, if I don't miss my guess. The red bromeliads have very dark green, pointed or lacinated leaves that look like a porcupine with her spines up."

Thrilled, Ari looked intently as the houseboat floated past the tree. "Wow...I see it! I wish we could stop and I could go climb the tree...." And then she laughed. "Of course, I'm scared to death of heights! I don't know what I'm going to do about that. I know a lot of orchids grow in the branches of trees."

Rafe chuckled. "The Juma will help you gather the ones you want. Besides, a lot of orchids are found on tree trunks or on rotting logs that have fallen to the earth. I don't think you'll want for orchids."

Ari couldn't sit still, she was so excited. Pushing her fingers through her hair to tame it into some semblance of smoothness, she confided in a low, hushed voice, "Rafe, I'm just afraid I'm in a beautiful dream. I'm afraid I'm going to wake up and it will be gone."

Chapter Five

It was early evening when Rafe moved the houseboat snugly in the calm, muddy channel. Rays of sunlight shot like spokes on a wheel through the gathering cauliflower-shaped clouds on the western horizon.

"These channels are known as *igarapes*," Rafe told Ari as he placed the plank from the houseboat to the earthen bank of the channel which was about forty-feet wide. "You'll see banana trees everywhere, palms, embauba trees, mangos and lots of coffee bushes." He grinned and leaped to the shore, then stepped halfway up the well-worn, partially painted plank. Holding out his hand to Ari, he said, "Welcome to my humble abode—the Amazon jungle, *señorita*."

Ari didn't know where to look first. As she turned to Rafe, she couldn't help but smile. He seemed so proud and confident. She stared at the hand he held out to her; it was large with long, artistic fingers, the nails blunt cut, and calluses across his palm. This was a man who worked in nature. Indeed, she thought as she leaned forward, placed her foot on the plank and slid her slender fingers into his, he seemed more and more like the Green Man of European myths and legends. The Green Man was nature personified. Someone who was in complete harmony with all around him.

"Thank you, Senor Antonio," she said in fluent Spanish. His fingers were strong and firm, yet it was obvious he monitored the amount of strength he exerted as he held her hand and guided her down the rickety plank. As she stepped foot on the reddish-colored earth, she gazed around at Rafe's camp.

There was a hammock strung between two mango trees and a circular pit for a fire nearby, with four smoothly cut logs around it that acted as chairs. A black iron tripod was set up over the pit, with an iron kettle suspended from it. A few feet away was a gray canvas tent. The tent was large, and she could see boxes and other items stowed within it. A well-worn footpath that led directly into the jungle.

Reluctant to release his hand, she came to Rafe's side and eased her fingers from him. "I'm here," she whispered in awe, "I'm really *here.*"

"And the beings of the jungle welcome you," Rafe said. He enjoyed her wonder, the hope burning eloquently in her face as she slowly took in every leaf, tree and bush that grew around the small encampment. Her face glowed with excitement. The jungle was alive with noises announcing the coming dusk. Crickets sang. Frogs croaked. In the distance, monkeys were chattering and alternately screaming and whooping at one another as they found their nests in the arms of trees for the coming night.

Heart swelling with joy, Ari turned when she saw something out of the corner of her eye. A small man, wrinkled and thin, his ribs pronounced above the dark green loincloth he wore, appeared silently out of the jungle on the footpath, his feet bare. He was old and his weathered features reminded her of an ancient oak tree. His eyes were dark brown, and his hair was thin and gray. When he met and held her gaze, he smiled. Ari couldn't help but smile back. The old man had most of his front teeth missing. She wondered how he was able to eat. In his hands, he held something about the size of a cantaloupe wrapped in red cloth. She noticed he wore several strands of seed necklaces interspersed with parrot feathers around his thin, wrinkled neck.

"Ah, Aroka," Rafe told her conspiratorially. "He's the chief of the Juma village. Come, you must meet him."

"How did he know we'd arrived?"

Grinning, Rafe slid his hands into hers and brought her along with him. The gesture was automatic. The look in Ari's eyes was one of acceptance and happiness, if he wasn't mistaken. Around her,

Rafe was finding that he was becoming completely instinctive and spontaneous. His head warned him that he shouldn't give in so easily to his desires, but his heart, so lonely and so long without a woman who loved this incredible jungle as he did, said it was perfectly all right. Rafe deferred to his heart— at least this one time. He couldn't help it—he was enchanted by Ari's happiness at being here.

Ari saw Aroka smile even more broadly as they halted in front of him. He spoke in an Indian language she didn't understand. As he spoke, he looked directly at her.

Rafe reluctantly released Ari's hand and stood between them, acting as interpreter. "Chief Aroka is officially welcoming you to his village. He has invited us to have dinner with him and his family tonight. Today he caught and killed a wild pig, which has been roasting all day in your honor. He says that you look like the sun goddess and wonders if your hair glows at night."

Ari laughed gently and reached out and touched the chief's shoulder. "Tell him I'm afraid not. Thank him. Can we go eat with them?"

Rafe swallowed his complete surprise. He hadn't expected Ari to be so willing to socialize with the natives just yet. "Of course. Half the time I'm eating with the chief and his family, anyway. If it wasn't for his wife, I'd starve at times."

Aroka nodded as Rafe accepted the invitation. The old man's pleasure was mirrored in his tobacco brown features, but then he lost his smile and began a solemn speech to Ari.

Rafe smiled a little and translated. ''The chief knows that you have come to draw the many orchids that live in the Great Mother Goddess's breast. He says that he had a dream last night, before you arrived. This gift he brings to you in welcoming you to his humble village, was what was shown to him by the goddess. He consulted his medicine woman, a priestess of the Jaguar Clan, and she said to present you with this orchid upon your arrival.''

Ari gasped. ''An orchid?'' She had to stop herself from reaching out for it. Aroka saw her hesitate, and laughed. Bowing deeply, he handed her the gift, which was wrapped in the frayed, red cotton cloth.

The instant the bundle settled in her hands, Ari quickly pulled away the cloth, which fluttered to the ground. What she held in her hands made her give a cry of joy. Of surprise.

''Oh, Rafe! Look! Look at this! Isn't it exquisite? Beautiful?''

The woman I'm looking at is exquisite and beautiful. Rafe bit back the words. Where had they come from? Instead, he said, ''It is.'' His voice was strained.

Gazing up at him, Ari drowned in the cinnamon warmth of his gaze and the gentle, hesitant smile he gave her. Instantly, she felt heat charge up her neck and flood her face. She was blushing badly, and her heart pounded at his sincere look. Tearing her gaze from his, she found the words choked in her throat, felt terribly shy in his suddenly larger-than-life presence.

Rafe realized he'd sounded less than enthusiastic. Her crestfallen expression squeezed his pounding heart. "Please," he urged her, "look at the beauty of the chief's gift. This is a *Gustavia august* orchid. The family is *Leychidacea*." The pink color on the petals reminded him of her blush, the white of the color of her skin.

Grateful, Ari stared down at the orchid that filled her hand. The leaves were oval, thick and leathery. There were two blooms on the orchid, one fully open, the other partially. The blooms reminded her of roses in shape and color, the pink ranging from fuschia to pale pink at the bottom of the petals. Intermixed with the pink was white and, at the base of each petal, a glaze of pale yellow. The center of the orchid held hundreds of tiny white filigree stamens that arced and bowed toward the deep gold center. Her hands grew hot holding the flower and tingles raced up her fingers and into her forearms. She felt as if in a dream; she was *living* a dream. Her mother's dream.

So much came flowing gently back to Ari as she stood between the two men on that bank while dusk softly approached. The shock that she was really here in the Amazon Basin living the dream she and her mother had planned suddenly overcame Ari. Tears welled in her eyes and quickly streaked down her face, dribbling off her chin as she reverently held the orchid in her hands.

"This—this is too much," she said in a choked voice. "Please...thank Chief Aroka. I never expected such a beautiful, incredible gift. I really didn't...."

Rafe laughed pleasantly and eased his hand across her slumped shoulders. He couldn't help but touch her because her fears overwhelmed his protective heart. "Well, get used to it, my wild woman. Down here in Amazonia, the Indians are the most generous people in the world. They will do anything for you. They will feed you, clothe you, even if they are starving and have no clothes to wear themselves. Such is the nature of their generosity and heart."

As Rafe slid his hand in a comforting gesture across her shoulders, Ari sniffed and balanced the huge orchid in her left hand. The white roots, a promise of new growth, looked like thick, gleaming worms beneath it. "Thanks, Rafe. Sorry I'm crying. It's just all a little overwhelming...."

Taking a linen handkerchief from his back pocket, he placed it in her right hand. "I understand, *mi rainha.*" Rafe chided himself for the Portuguese endearment. It meant "my queen." Being around Ari was disconcerting. It was as if he were no longer in control of his well-ordered world.

Ari blotted her eyes and apologized profusely to the chief. She wondered what Rafe had said to her in his own tongue. Whatever it was, she saw that his eyes had softened.

"Aroka says it is good to cry. He says it pleases the rain gods and goddesses."

Sniffing and wiping her nose a final time, Ari stuffed his handkerchief into the pocket of her jeans. "Tell him that his gift is priceless to me. It will be the first orchid that I'll try to draw. I know it won't be any good, but I'm so inspired by its beauty." She held it up for Rafe to observe. "Look at it! Doesn't it seem otherworldly to you? As if it is just a visitor to our world?"

Chuckling, Rafe said, "The Indians believe that orchids are very ancient teachers to us all, if we will only sit and listen to them. As you know, orchids don't need any soil to live or grow in. All they need—" he gestured toward the jungle and the apricot-colored clouds above them as the sun set "—is air and humidity. No other plant on the face of Mother Earth can do that. So, yes, they are special. Far more special and unique than most people suspect."

As Ari held the orchid, she felt transported. All she wanted to do was sit quietly with this plant and communicate with it by drawing it. She knew from past experience that when she drew, she entered an altered state of consciousness. The outer world would fall away and there was only her, the colors, the textures and the scent of the orchid. It was a time she always looked forward to, as if the true gift was being able to walk across that invisible bridge of energy and light and be in communion with the spirit of the orchid itself.

"Yes," she whispered unsteadily, "I know exactly what you mean."

"I thought you might," Rafe murmured. He saw a number of other Indians, all members of Aroka's immediate family, coming down the path to greet them. "Well, I've got some work to do for a few minutes. Why don't you put your new friend below, in the galley? I'll tidy up around here and then we'll go back with the chief and his family and have some pig for dinner."

Overwhelmed with so much going on all at once, Ari was glad for his advice. She spoke in Spanish to Aroka and politely excused herself. He nodded, bowed and grinned, though she wasn't sure he understood her. Scrambling up the plank, Ari was captured by the drama unfolding in the sky around them. The once white, frayed-looking cumulus clouds that haunted the jungle, hanging hundreds of feet above the triple canopy, had turned from a peach color to a deep orange hue with a fringing of crimson along their edges. The sky was no longer blue, but a soft whitish color that was quickly being chased away by inky looking darkness. Magical…yes, this place was pure magic. Ari almost thought that if she willed the clouds to change shape, they would; such was the thrumming power that swirled around her, embraced her and made her feel part of all things in this magnificent place called Amazonia.

Ari awoke slowly the next morning, her face pressed deeply into the small goose down pillow. As she moved from her stomach to her back, the light cotton sheet and thin blanket felt much too warm to her. Shoving them away, she untangled the knee-length, violet silk nightgown she wore. What time was it? From the depths of the houseboat, she heard a cricket singing its heart out. Smiling sleepily, she realized that the faint light of dawn was filtering down through the opened hatch above the wooden stairs. Looking at her watch, blinking away the sleep from her eyes, Ari saw that it was 6:00 a.m.

Groaning, she pushed herself upward. This was the first day of her life. *Her* life. Not her father's, but her own. As she placed her bare feet on the cool teakwood deck, she stretched languidly and smiled. Other sounds drifted into her consciousness. Her stomach rumbled. Laughing softly, she got to her feet. She shouldn't be hungry at all! The chief's wife had urged her to eat and then eat some more. Everyone had poked at her ribs and told her she was too skinny, saying that in a thunderstorm, the wind goddess would carry her away. They'd all had many laughs over Ari's thinness. And she'd dutifully eaten more than her fill. Of course, Rafe didn't help things by agreeing with the Jumas.

What a wonderful night she'd had with Aroka and his family. She'd loved sitting outside their thatched hut, around the coals of the campfire, sharing the delicious meal of wild pig.

As Ari emerged from the toilet, she picked up her brush and ran it through the thick, golden strands of her hair. Today *was* the first day of her life. That awareness thrummed through her once more, quiet and yet strong and filled with brimming vibrancy.

She could hardly wait to get dressed and start sketching the orchid that sat on the table across from her makeshift bed.

Climbing into a pair of jeans, a deep-pink tank top and a pair of hiking boots, Ari quickly brushed her teeth and tamed her flyaway hair into a semblance of order. She hurried up the creaking stairs, and as she emerged from the hold, she gasped. Above the quiet, muddy Amazon and the dark green jungle, the sky was alive with brilliant, swirling colors. Mouth falling open, Ari became momentarily lost in the pale peach, the deeper apricot and the fragile lavender hues near the eastern horizon, where the sun had yet to rise.

This morning the gauzy white clouds created by the constant humidity of the fertile rain forest below were like pale orange curtains languidly spreading and rippling across the light blue background. She stood, almost frozen, her hands on the rails at the top of the hatch, just allowing the colors to filter through her like nonstop energy. Lifting her chin, she closed her eyes and absorbed the other sounds—the call of birds awakening now that the sun was about to arrive. The screech of monkeys. The final croaks of nearby frogs.

Sweet scents—of orchids, she was sure—wafted into her nostrils. And then she caught another whiff, this time, of bacon and eggs and coffee. How was that possible? Opening her eyes, Ari twisted to look to her left. There, hunched over the campfire and holding a huge black skillet in hand, was Rafe. Her heart swelled. He was watching her, a soft hint of a smile tugging at the corners of his wonderfully shaped male mouth. Why was it that every time he looked at her she felt giddy, delicious and beautiful? No man had ever made her feel like that.

Leaping to the deck, Ari hurried down the plank and jogged to where he stood. "Good morning," she whispered. "Can I do anything to help you?"

Rafe enjoyed the drowsy look in Ari's wide blue eyes. What a change in her from yesterday! It was like night and day. She was relaxed now, and her happiness was evident in the sparkling gold flecks deep in her blue eyes, the soft, lush smile on her lips and the way she held herself. Today her shoulders weren't as slumped. And she was able to hold eye contact with him longer.

"Good morning. No, just have a seat here." He motioned to one of the smooth logs that doubled as a chair. "I've got scrambled eggs, lots of bacon and some fresh coffee ready for you."

"I'm feeling very spoiled," she said, laughing as she sat down. "This is wonderful! Thank you." Rafe had placed two plastic plates with flatware on the log. There were salt and pepper shakers nearby.

Moving the bacon around with the fork over the low flame, Rafe decided that Ari was nothing like Justine. She actually enjoyed being here in his camp. The discovery was a pleasant shock to him. Setting the skillet on the coals, he rose and picked up the battered, blackened tin coffeepot. Ari handed him a tin mug. He poured the steaming, fragrant coffee into it and handed it back to her. She passed him a second one and he filled it and placed it on the log nearby.

As Ari raised the coffee to her lips, she saw large, bright red birds skimming the surface of the Amazon barely a hundred feet away. "What are those?"

Rafe turned. "*Guara.* Scarlet ibis. Beautiful, aren't they?"

Gasping, she counted at least twenty of them. "Gorgeous! What a bright color against the chocolate brown of the Amazon and the deep green of the jungle."

"Spoken like a true artist," Rafe said with a smile as he divvied up the bacon and eggs between the two plates. "You see things in terms of color, light and hues. I like that."

Sighing, Ari watched the unfolding of the sky's colors. "You're right. I never realized that until just now. Look at the dawn. I've never seen anything like this anywhere. Ever."

Rafe handed her a plate and flatware. "Get use to it. Amazonia has her own special magic that she works on those who visit her. In time, she'll cast her spell on you, and you'll never want to leave." He sat down near her, but not near enough to make Ari feel uncomfortable. Setting his coffee cup on the ground next to his boot, he dug into the scrambled eggs with relish.

Sighing, Ari followed his lead. She salted her eggs, realizing once again how hungry she was. As they sat there, eating in silence, the sounds that surrounded them were melodic and caressing. Facing the slow-moving Amazon River and watching the bird population come to life as the sun broached the horizon was all Ari wanted. She saw scarlet-and-gold macaws flying rapidly from one side of the river to the other, always in that squadronlike formation. And then she saw another flight of smaller green-and-red parrots fly over their camp.

"Color…it's everywhere," Ari said reverently as she caught Rafe's gaze. He was wolfing down his large breakfast. She was picking slowly at her food, too excited by all that she was absorbing into her heart and soul to eat, despite her rumbling stomach. "I know my mother would have cried to see this. I had no idea how beautiful Amazonia really is. Books can paint word pictures, but to be here, to feel *her*…"

He smiled a little. "Yes, it's a her. You feel her, don't you?"

Giving him a confused look, Ari picked up a bit of bacon and chewed thoughtfully on it. "What *is* it, Rafe? What's this feeling I sense in and around me? I've never had this sensation before. Am I crazy? Is it my wild imagination taking off again?"

Chuckling, he picked up his coffee and took a sip. Setting it back down at his feet, he said, "No. The Indians call it *onca,* jaguar energy. Onca is Portuguese for Jaguar. It is said that the jaguar is the queen of the jungle and she rules it in the name of Mother Earth. Jaguar energy is said to be alive and fertile—more powerful than any other energy or animal anywhere in the world."

"It almost feels like there's an invisible river flowing slowly through and around me."

Nodding, Rafe said, "Yes."

"And everyone can feel or sense this?"

"Everyone I know does." And then he smiled. "But then, my life is here in Amazonia, with the Indians. They are very sensitive to this energy. They can tell you when there is an *onca*, jaguar, nearby. Each village has a jaguar priest or priestess. There is the Jaguar Clan, which is steeped in mystery and myths that go back hundreds, thousands of years, from what I can tell from my conversations with the Indians. Information about this mysterious and powerful clan is carried down to each new generation by word of mouth. Nothing has ever been written about the clan, or the people who train to work with jaguar medicine and energy."

Her eyes widened. "I must go get my journal. You're telling me so many wonderful stories! I don't want to miss a word of it, Rafe." She quickly set her breakfast aside and trotted back to the houseboat.

Chuckling indulgently, Rafe enjoyed watching Ari. She was an excited child. Yet she moved like a lithe gazelle, or maybe one of those blue or white herons that lived in the hundreds of *igarapes* along the Amazon river. He felt his heart swell with so many good feelings. Putting his own plate aside, he picked up his coffee and simply enjoyed the coming dawn. He hadn't realized how lonely he'd become without the presence of a woman, until now.

Sipping the dark, fragrant coffee, Rafe didn't try

to fool himself. He was deeply drawn to Ari, to her innocence, to her idealistic view of life and the world around her. She was an artist to her soul. He could see that in the way color affected her. The hues that changed minute by minute here in Amazonia brought so many sweet expressions to her mobile features. He found himself absorbing her wonder like a thirsty sponge. Shaking his head, he realized that the Indians would say that the *onca* had brought him his mate. And of course, *onca* mated only once, for life. Then he caught himself. That Ari could be his mate was a ridiculous thought. After the debacle with Justine, Rafe had sworn off finding a woman. He had accepted that he would always be a loner.

Life was precious to Rafe. He lived in the moment, for at any time, he could be killed by a miner or drug runner's bullet. Every day was like a feast before him and he wanted to take full advantage of each new dawn. He normally embraced life completely, without apology or hesitation—except when it came to women. No, they were to be approached slowly and with respect.

Though Ari was someone he wanted to know more intimately, he shoved that desire aside. Completely. Still, his body ached with the ripening awareness that he wanted to touch her. What would it be like to run his fingers through the strands of her golden hair? They had felt silky and strong tangled around his fingertips yesterday. She invited his touch. Her skin was like that of a soft, ripe peach and he wanted to explore every inch of her with kisses, the lick of his tongue, indulging and losing himself in her womanly fragrance. More than anything, he felt his heart clamoring loudly to own up to his feelings about her. How could he? Ari was here to live out a dream for herself and her mother. And that was *all* she was here for.

Rafe heard her skipping down the plank. Lifting his head, he watched as she made her way back to where he sat. He remembered how she had hesitated earlier to come down the rickety and somewhat wobbly plank. This time she practically sailed down without apprehension. Yes, that was good. Ari was already learning to not be so afraid of the world around her. In fact, she was emboldened in her new surroundings and he knew why: he was supporting her as she stepped out of her normal, scared self, so that she could clasp life in both hands, instead.

He watched as she plopped down next to him breathless, and quickly opened her journal. Painstakingly, she took her pen, wrote down the day and the time. Silence lulled them as she began to pen the story of the *onca* goddess. Her handwriting was precise, with a flowery edge to it.

"I wish my handwriting was as easy to read as yours," Rafe said. "My boss back at headquarters gripes all the time, when he gets my sweat-stained reports, that my hen scratching is like a doctor's scrawl."

Ari grinned. "I'm not surprised your reports are sweaty, I can feel the humidity in the air." She lifted one hand and touched the other palm. "My hands are already damp."

"Mmm, the humidity is usually at its highest in the morning hours. As the sun rises, it will lower. We're in the dry season, fall, anyway, which is good if you want to sketch the orchids. Come winter, it will rain all day and night, almost nonstop. The Amazon will rise and flood out this area completely."

"Really?" Ari looked around, impressed.

"Yes, so you'd better plan on getting most of your orchids drawn in the next three months."

"I love the rain," Ari said softly, returning to her journal. "I could hunt for orchids, bring them back to the houseboat and draw down below, couldn't I?"

The thought of having her for longer than three months made him uneasy. How he wished Ari would stay that long, but the reasonable side of his nature, the pragmatic side, told him she would more than likely leave sooner rather than later. "Yes," he said, "you could. I can string some lights above the table for you. I've got a small gasoline generator in the engine room that can be fired up and used on days like that. You'll need good light to draw."

Ari reached out, her fingers sliding along Rafe's dark, hairy forearm. His flesh was hard and warm beneath her fingertips. She saw his eyes suddenly darken, like the sky as a storm gathered. His lips parted slightly in reaction to her unexpected touch. She couldn't help herself, nor did she want to where Rafe was concerned. "You're such a wonderful knight in shining armor to me." Her voice lowered.

"And you're so thoughtful. I—I just never expected this…or you…and I feel like I'm in this wonderful, unfolding dream filled with beauty and love…."

Love. The word was like a brand burning into his heart. As Ari softly touched his arm, an electric feeling moved wildly up through him, and Rafe could no longer think. She was so spontaneous, this wild, natural woman of his, that he was constantly caught off guard by her. He knew his heart was in danger, but he was helpless against the flow of feelings she conjured in him. Powerless in the face of her innocent affection—sweet feelings that would one day surely burn them both.

Chapter Six

Ari was just putting the finishing touches on her first orchid portrait when she heard shouts and cries from the Amazon River. Rafe had set up a small table and chair for her beneath the long, wide leaves of a two-year-old banana tree near the jungle's edge, away from the path to the Juma village. She faced the river so that she could see all the colorful birds that were in constant flight across it. The spot provided shade as well as privacy, and she had wanted to be alone to draw. But she was glad she was close enough to where Rafe performed his daily activities. Putting her colored pencil aside, Ari raised her chin toward the sounds coming from the camp.

She could see three dugout canoes coming into the *igarape*. Rafe emerged from the houseboat and lifted his hand in greeting as he spoke in the Indian language to the men in loincloths, who paddled their canoes to the bank in order to disembark. Like all the Indians Ari had met so far, these men were very short compared to Rafe, who towered over them.

With a sigh, she thought about all that she'd encountered in the seven days since coming to Amazonia. Her life had slowed down to vivid moments with animals, visits with the Indian people or hours drawing her first orchid for the book. More than anything, Ari admitted to herself, Rafe's constant company was what she desired. She derived great pleasure in watching him work, whether he was talking with the Indian leaders constantly coming and going from his campsite, or wrestling with a mountain of paperwork, which, he admitted, he hated doing.

Most of all, Ari enjoyed the moments alone with Rafe. They traded off cooking duties. One day she would cook, the next day he would. Doing dishes at night in the hold of the houseboat, standing elbow to elbow with him at the drain board, was a secret thrill to her. She *liked* touching Rafe "accidentally." And despite her lack of experience with men, she knew what it meant when his eyes darkened perceptibly as she brushed his arm with her own. If she was any judge, he enjoyed the pleasurable accidents, too.

When Ari saw a man dressed like a chief, with macaw feathers draped around his neck, leap out of the prow of one dugout canoe as soon as the bow touched the bank, she knew something was wrong.

The chief was talking rapidly, his voice stressed, as he hurried toward Rafe, who was walking down the plank to greet them.

Ari saw the grimness on the faces of the other warriors, who disembarked and pulled their canoes partly up on the bank. Dressed in loincloths because of the heat and humidity, they carried blowguns, machetes in leather sheaths at their sides, as well what looked like two very old rifles, with them. This was the first time Ari had seen armed Indians. Frowning, she sat up, watching alertly from her table. Rafe invited them to sit down at the campfire. There was always a greeting ceremony, and Rafe was respectful of each tribe's protocols. He poured them coffee, and Ari watched as they eagerly dumped several heaping spoonfuls of white sugar into their cups, knowing that sugar was a rare treat for the Indians.

Ari knew enough to keep out of Rafe's business. Many times she'd seen him act as a peacemaker between two tribal nations. She enjoyed watching him use his hands, his cajoling deep voice and facial expressions to get disagreeing parties to cooperate with one another in order to keep the peace within his district. He was a man of honor. A knight who cared and protected the people in his domain.

Distracted by the sight of the men in the distance, but not wanting to intrude on them, Ari decided to take a walk. It was an hour until lunch. She felt happy with the completion of her first orchid drawing. Oh, the quality was nothing to write home about, but she was pleased with her effort. Leaving her table where the orchid and her sketchbook lay, she wandered down the trail toward the Juma village.

Rafe stood with his hands propped tensely on his hips as Chief Mulki and his men paddled away from the camp. Turning, he caught sight of Ari emerging from the path. For a brief moment, the sun peeked out from behind the cottony cumuli overhead and the beams seemed to set her hair on fire like gold being melted at high heat. Did she know how beautiful she was? Today she wore a pale pink, cotton camisole with delicate lace that outlined her upper body to perfection, and khaki slacks that emphasized her wide hips. Hips, he realized, that could easily carry and birth a baby. Frowning, he wondered where that thought had come from. In Amazonia, the Indian women gave birth naturally, in their huts. They had no clinic or medical facilities nearby. And there were no cesarean sections, either. Rafe had learned, over the years, that a woman with wide hips would birth easily. Those with narrower hips always had long, agonizing births instead.

As Ari saw him and smiled shyly in his direction, he felt his heart expand with joy. It would be easy to imagine Ari loving him, having his babies and raising them with him in the wilds of Amazonia, truly free and natural. Rubbing his wrinkled brow, he tried to erase those nagging thoughts, but they were like delicious nectar being sipped out of an orchid. He couldn't imagine such a life with her. He feared too much that she would lure him away from the Amazon and everything that he held as dear. After all, she'd only just come here from her comfortable life in the States. Her wonder with this land could be short-lived.

Besides, Ari deserved someone who wasn't a rogue like himself. She needed someone who was willing to live the same conventional and privileged life-style she'd come from. No, he was a lone warrior fighting overwhelming odds out here in Amazonia, and he could offer Ari none of those things. Coming from a moneyed and powerful family, she would never be satisfied with his Spartan life-style, anyway. He couldn't trust that her love for Amazonia would last—especially considering the world she had left behind.

As he watched her approach, Rafe silently applauded Ari's new posture. Now she walked with her chin up most of the time and her shoulders drawn back with newly found esteem, instead of rounded as before. The changes in her over the past week were startling and invigorating to him. It was like watching a butterfly emerge from her imprisoning cocoon and grow into a beautiful creature before his eyes.

As Ari approached, Rafe reached out. "Come and sit down, I've got some bad news," he told her. As his hand made contact with hers, he saw her eyes grow soft with desire. When her fingers curled around his with equal firmness, Rafe had to stop himself from drawing her fully against him and kissing her senseless.

"Bad news?" Ari asked, alarmed. Rafe still held her hand as she sat down next to him on the log facing the campfire. She waited for such moments with him; the natural intimacy that connected them powerfully to one another leaped to life like a lightning bolt flashing between them. Abruptly, he released her hand, as if realizing he was holding it far too long. Ari felt sad; she liked contact with him.

"Yes. Chief Mulki was just here with some of his warriors. He lives about ten miles downstream, at the edge of my territory." Rafe motioned in that general direction. "One of his nephews just got captured by a drug lord. He's probably being taken to one of the cocaine factories deep in the jungle, to work as a slave laborer there."

Compressing her lips, Ari held Rafe's worried gaze. "You said this happened often."

"Yes," he said unhappily. "Too often."

"And his life's in danger?"

"It might be," Rafe hedged, seeing the darkness of fear stalking her wide blue eyes. "I promised the chief I'd leave in the skiff today and go downriver and investigate. Usually, when this happens, the person—child or adult—is never seen again. They're put in chains to do the work in the factories during the day, and at night they're herded with other captured Indians into a fenced prison—barbed wire with concertina strung across the top of it—so they can't escape. And if they do try to escape, they're shot dead." With a shake of his head, Rafe muttered, "Very few have come back to tell us about these things. I wish my country would mount a military effort, work with the Indians and attack these factories. I know where several of them are.'' Frustration lined his voice. ''If I went in there alone to try and free any Indians, I'd be killed long before I ever reached a facility. The drug lords have guards posted miles away from the factories. No one has been able to make a dent in these illegal operations.''

Rubbing his hands against the khaki material on his thighs, he added, ''I'm going to have to leave you here alone while I go investigate.''

''I'll be okay,'' Ari said. ''I know my way around now.'' She felt her heart squeeze in terror for his safety. She would miss him terribly. Ari had come to cherish their time together.

He eyed her. ''I know you do, but I'll worry.''

She smiled a little. ''Chief Aroka and his warriors will protect me.''

Rafe reached out and tamed several golden flyaway strands that lifted in the humid breeze sweeping ashore from the river, tucking them gently behind her delicate ear. Watching her eyes grow warm and lustrous, he stopped himself from further intimacy with her. ''The drug runners and the drug lords' soldiers usually stay away from my camp. They give it a wide berth. Chief Mulki was saying that he's heard they are looking for more slaves for their factories, so things could get unsettled in a hurry.''

''No place is safe?'' Ari asked as she absorbed his fleeting touch. How she ached to kiss him! It was a dark, mesmerizing obsession with her. Every night, in bed, Ari wondered what it would be like to kiss Rafe's very male, yet tender mouth. Forcing herself to stop staring at his lips, she looked up into his stormy, narrowed eyes. Her heart pounded briefly, for she'd seen that look before, usually when they were washing dishes at the sink together.

Rafe didn't want to admit she was right about the danger. He was finding that Ari could be a worrywart upon occasion. Usually she would stop being anxious once she understood or experienced whatever it was that was new and frightening to her. But as flexible as she was, Ari wouldn't be able to handle the anxieties his absence might cause. Folding his hands between his opened thighs, he leaned his elbows on them. "I've got a plan," he said, giving her a slight smile. "From all our conversations the past week, I can see you really miss having a big sister in your life. While I'm gone, I'm going to ask a close friend of mine, Inca, to come and stay with you."

"How long will you be gone?" Ari tried to keep the worry out of her voice, but it was impossible. Rafe was going into a dangerous situation.

Shrugging, he murmured, "I don't know, Ari. I wish I could tell you. I'll need to start tracking the kidnapped nephew. I'll get help from the Indians, but it could mean days, even a week, before we find something, a clue...."

"Oh..." She suddenly felt anxiety. "And Inca? She's your friend? A backwoodsman?"

He laughed. "Inca is Inca. She's the mistress of Amazonia."

"Wait," Ari said, holding out her hand. "I heard Chief Aroka talking about her. Is she the one they call the jaguar goddess?"

Rafe held her wide, awed gaze. "Inca is called many things by many people. To her friends, she is loyal and would die for them. Her enemies would like to hang her head on a pike. The Brazilian government has a large monetary reward for her capture. They say she's murdered thirteen people, but that's not true. Inca would never murder. She would fire in defense, however, and I'm sure that's what happened, regardless of what her enemies say."

"Whew," Ari whispered. "The jaguar goddess here? With me?"

"You'll like her. She's terribly human," Rafe reassured her. "Inca is a good role model for you, Ari. She's strong, confident and very sure of herself. And on top of that, she's a woman." His voice lowered with reverence. "An incredible, heart-centered woman. She's saved my neck more than a few times, believe me."

"How old is she?"

"Twenty-six, I think. About your age. I'm sure you'll get along famously. Besides, Inca knows where some of the most exotic orchids in this jungle grow. No one knows Amazonia better than Inca. She's constantly traversing the basin, protecting her people and giving them aid. I'm sure she'll be a wonderful guide for you."

Heartened, Ari said, "Are you sure she won't be bored out of her skull with the likes of me?"

Laughing, Rafe said, "How can you say that about yourself? I find you the most fascinating person I've ever met." He motioned to her table beneath the shade of the banana tree. "You have an artist's temperament and you see the world around you in colors. Inca has never met an artist before. I think she'll be intrigued by your talent, by your heart."

Flushing, Ari looked forlornly at the sketchpad that she'd shut before leaving it on her work table. "I think when Inca sees my primitive work, she'll die laughing. A child could do better than me."

Her glumness moved him. "Let me look at it. I'll decide for myself."

Her heart thudded with fear. "No! I mean…I usually don't show my drawings to anyone…."

"Why not? Your mother taught you to draw. What did she say about your efforts?" Rafe saw her newly found self-esteem leak out of her like air from a punctured balloon. Moments before, confidence had emanated from her. It was a fragile confidence, but at least it was there and growing within her. Now her face carried an expression of shame. Who had made her feel like this about her work? Her self-expression? Intuitively, he knew it was her father, who derided everything she did that wasn't what he wanted her to do.

Throwing her hands up nervously, Ari uttered in desperation, "My mom always encouraged me." She chewed on her lip, silent for a long time. Finally, she confessed, "I feel uneasy about showing you my work."

Following his heart, Rafe moved closer and slid his arm around her slumped shoulders. She sat as if beaten, like a cowering dog—the same demeanor he'd seen seven days ago at the airport in Manaus. "*Mi rainha*," he began gently, his arm closing around her and drawing her against him, "I will *never* laugh at your work. Creation comes from the heart. How can anyone judge that? Or laugh? Or make fun of your efforts? By now, you know I take your art seriously."

Closing her eyes, Ari gave in to him briefly. How strong and sure Rafe felt as he eased her against his tall, stalwart frame. Heart hammering, her mouth dry, she was speechless as a gamut of rainbow sensations raced through her. Being in his embrace was heaven! She felt safe. She felt worthy. She felt like she never had to apologize for herself or her art.

"Okay…" she blurted, and quickly pulled away from his arm as she rose. "Just this *one* time, Rafe. Okay?"

The desperation in her eyes and voice cut into his heart. "Of course," he agreed.

Frowning, she turned on her heel and went to fetch her sketchpad from the table. It took everything Ari had to sit back down, her elbow brushing his as she did. Her hands were clammy as she rested the pad across her lap. Fingers trembling badly, she lifted the heavy cardboard covering.

Rafe held his breath. Words exploded softly from

him as he gazed down upon her creation. "This…
this—it's exquisite, Ari!" He looked up at her, respect in his eyes. "That orchid looks real enough to
jump off the page at me." Staring at it, he saw the
ephemeral beauty of the pale yellow of the petal
flowing into the soft pink, and then growing into a
fuschia color at the outer edges. Without thinking,
he gently touched the edge of her sketchbook. "This
is beautiful. Simply, elegantly beautiful. I've *never*
seen anyone capture the spirit of an orchid as you
have." He studied her shocked features. "Your
heart, your soul, come through in this drawing, Ari.
Did you know that? That's why it appears so alive."

Incredulous at his praise, Ari felt heat rolling up
her neck and into her face. She saw the admiration
burning like a fire in his darkening eyes. He was
more animated than she'd ever seen him. Even more,
his velvet baritone voice was laced with emotion.
Once again, the difference between her cold, distant
father and the warmth and openness of Rafe overwhelmed Ari's being. She thrilled to his words and
saw that he meant every one of them.

"You—really think it's a good likeness?"

Laughing, Rafe reached out and embraced her
hard. For an instant, she froze, surprised at his gesture, but then she relaxed against him, the pad
clutched in her hands. Kissing her warm, tousled
hair, he whispered, "My wild woman of Amazonia,
you not only belong here, but you feel every particle
of the orchid children you draw with your heart.

These drawings are children of your heart, hands and eyes...."

Shaken and hungry for his continued attention, Ari lifted her chin. She met and held his dark, turbulent eyes as they narrowed upon her. Her breath hitched. He was going to kiss her. Nothing seemed so right. Nothing. Her hands loosened around the sketchpad and she found them moving of their own accord across his hard torso, lightly exploring his well-sprung rib cage beneath the soft dampness of his cotton shirt.

The odor of the campfire encircled her as he leaned down, his eyes pinned to hers. Her lips parted, and she raised her chin fractionally to meet his descending mouth. Automatically, her lashes swept downward. Anticipation flowed through her as milliseconds melted away. The first time his mouth brushed hers, she shuddered. But it wasn't out of fear; it was out of longing and need for him. Ari shyly returned his grazing touch as he tasted her lips as lightly as a butterfly tastes a flower. The scent of him, as a man, filled her flaring nostrils as he drew her more deeply into his arms, his hand guiding her face and angling it so he could take her more deeply this time.

The moment his mouth settled firmly on her lips, she yielded to his controlled strength. Lights exploded behind her closed eyes. Fire ignited within her lower body as his lips slid teasingly along her wet ones. Their breathing grew ragged. She felt a keen hunger as she strained upward to meet and match his cajoling kisses. Losing herself in the bright sunlight of his magnificent male body, the power of his mouth caressing and taking hers, Ari felt her spirit soar. Her heart was hammering in her breasts, her nipples sensitized as she grazed his chest with hers. The perfume of the orchids swirled around her. Rafe tasted of coffee, of the honey-covered bread he'd eaten earlier, all these combined with the scent of him as a man to entice her spiraling senses to new heights of awareness.

All too soon, she felt his mouth leave hers, and Ari moaned a little as he drew away from her. Looking up, she was mesmerized by the dark storm clouds in his eyes. She felt at once captured and preyed upon by him. But it wasn't fear that she felt. No, this sensation felt right. This was what it was like to be claimed by a powerful man, Ari thought, her mind still spinning, her thoughts a collage of bright, scintillating feelings.

"I'm sorry," Rafe told her huskily, "I had no right...to kiss you..." And he didn't. A gentleman did not take without asking first of a lady. What was happening to him? Was the danger ahead of him making him crazy? Was he afraid he would die and never taste the orchid sweetness of her soft, full lips? Die and never know? Was he scared of being torn from Ari without having shared how he really felt about her, despite their very different worlds?

Stunned, Ari couldn't find her voice. She gripped his lower arms with her hands and shook her head. The regret in his eyes, the apology, tore through her.

•

"No..." she whispered unsteadily. "No, it was good. It was right. Don't say you're sorry. Please don't..."

Sliding his fingers across her fiery cheek, he whispered, "No apologies, *mi flor,* my flower. Consider this a goodbye kiss until I can get back?"

Laying her cheek in his opened hand, Ari closed her eyes. She never wanted this moment to end. It was too exquisite. Rafe liked her drawing of the orchid. He liked *her* or he wouldn't have kissed her. "I've never been kissed like that before," she told him breathlessly. "It was so beautiful...."

"Sacred," Rafe whispered huskily as he watched her eyes open. "As soon as Inca arrives, I will leave. You will be as safe in her hands as mine."

"Indeed? More so in mine, *mi irmao,* my brother."

Ari gasped as the husky voice of a woman broke the tender moment. Jerking a look in the direction of the voice, her eyes grew huge.

Rafe grinned crookedly, released Ari and turned. Inca was standing less than six feet away from them. He hadn't heard her approach; but then, she was the jaguar goddess; she knew how to walk in complete silence, like the animal who was her guardian spirit. He met her willow-green eyes, which sparkled with amusement. As usual, she was in jungle camouflage fatigues and black army boots. A pair of bandoleers crossed her sleeveless olive-green T-shirt. In her right hand she carried her rifle, which he knew was never far from her grasp. Her hair, long, thick and black, was caught up in a single braid that hung lazily across her right shoulder.

"Inca..." Rafe said, rising and drawing Ari up with him. Rafe knew how intimidating Inca could be, but for whatever reason, he saw that she was shielding them from the usual thunderstorm of energy that always swirled around her. He saw Inca's eyes soften as her gaze fell on Ari. Yes, Inca understood instinctively that Ari was not the strong, powerful woman that she herself was.

Inca's full lips softened as she spoke. "So, you are the great artist I have heard about?" She began as she moved bonelessly around in front of them. Offering her hand to Ari, she continued, "My brother, Rafe, has high praise for you, Ari. I am Inca. It is an honor to meet you."

Ari stared up at the woman. She had never met anyone like her. Inca stood at least six feet tall, with a medium boned frame that was all lean muscle and firmness from her slender, golden arms to the curve of her long thighs. Her skin glowed from a slight film of perspiration, and it seemed to Ari as if life throbbed around her like a million suns shining all at once. Yet as Inca eased her hand forward, the sincere look of welcome in her eyes gave Ari the courage to slide her hand into hers.

"Hi, Inca." She felt the firmness of the woman's handshake. Releasing Inca's hand, she looked up at Rafe. "Are you brother and sister?"

Laughing huskily, Inca said, "No, but Rafe is *like* a brother to me." She reached over and embraced

Rafe quickly, then released him. "And I, his younger sister who is always around when he gets into trouble."

In his mind, Rafe cringed at her wording, because he knew it would only serve to upset Ari more.

Inca stepped back and amended her words by saying, "Rafe rarely gets into trouble, though, and I like to come and visit him. We play chess together. And I always win."

Unsure of Inca, who moved with such grace and confidence, Ari said little. She saw the warmth and care between this woman and Rafe. He looked relieved to see her.

Rafe slid his arm around Ari as they stood there. "I've got to go downriver."

"Yes, I heard," Inca said as she placed her rifle against the log and then divested herself of the bandoleers. Tugging her damp T-shirt back into place, she pulled the canteen from the web belt around her waist, unscrewed the top and lifted it to her lips. After taking a long drink, she recapped the canteen. "Go carefully, my brother. The Valentino Brothers are the men who took the nephew."

Nodding, Rafe muttered, "I thought so. Have you been able to pick up their tracks?"

Shaking her head, Inca shoved the canteen back into her belt. "No. I had to be elsewhere." Looking down at Ari, Inca grew thoughtful. "I can stay here until you return. There is nothing that pressing for me, right now."

"Good," Rafe said, inwardly relieved. Inca wasn't always available. As a matter of fact, Amazonia was her territory. *All* of it. Inca was superhuman in some ways and the Indian people desperately needed the healing and protection she supplied them with.

Inca smiled slightly and moved over to the log. "This is your sketchbook, Ari?" she asked, scooping the pad up. "May I look at it?"

Panic struck Ari. Before she could say no, Inca had carefully opened the pad and was looking hard at her drawing. Words of protest jammed in Ari's throat. She stood there, feeling helpless and trying to protect herself against Inca's rejection of her work.

Inca slowly turned her head, her gaze locking with Ari's frightened one. "Why do you cringe when someone gazes upon the beauty of your skills?" She tapped the drawing. "You have captured the otherworldliness of the orchid. Has she not, my brother?"

Rafe felt Ari sag a little, all the tension bleeding out of her once she realized Inca liked the drawing, too. "Yes, Ari has captured the heart and soul of our orchid people."

Eyes gleaming, Inca handed Ari the closed sketchbook. "You must let me go with you. I want to watch you create. I have never seen anyone draw or paint as well as you do. It will be an honor to help you find some beautiful orchids for your book. Your mother will be very pleased."

Shaken, Ari looked up at Rafe and then back at Inca. Had Rafe talked to Inca of her past? Her mother? The reason why Ari was here in the first place? She saw Rafe's lips part, his brows drop, but he said nothing. Giving Inca a strange look, Ari almost asked Inca if she could read minds, but decided against it. Suddenly Ari felt a little intimidated by Inca. The woman was a leader, there was no doubt. The way she carried herself, the way she held her chin at a proud angle, and the way she spoke showed her confidence. There was firmness, power and conviction behind her words. Although Inca's English was rudimentary, Ari noted as she turned to Rafe to speak more privately, she was fluent in Spanish and Portuguese. Ari was able to interpret some of what they said, but not all of it.

"I will guard her, my brother," Inca said, dropping into Portuguese.

"Good. She needs a role model like you."

Inca grinned wickedly. "Your soft little rabbit will turn into a jaguar by the time you return. Then what will you do?"

Rafe returned her grin with one of his own. "Revel in it. As you can see, she's a shadow of herself."

"I see much. Do not worry. You will be gone at least seven days. When you return, your flower will have blossomed even more."

Rafe reached out and gripped Inca's proud shoulder. "Thank you, my sister. I don't know how you do it—you are here for so many—but I'm grateful to you for helping me."

"Humph. Go, before I break down in tears." Inca smiled and gripped his arm in a gesture of friendship. "I will send a spirit guide with you. Where you go, the dark forces gather."

"Thanks, I'll take all the help anyone can give

me,'' he told her. Rafe reluctantly turned to Ari. ''I've got to go now. Inca knows her way around here. Anything you need, just ask her.''

Feeling bereft as Rafe left her side, Ari stood there helplessly. Inca came and stood nearby, watching with her as Rafe mounted the plank to the houseboat. ''Little sister, do not worry so much. He is in the hands of the Great Mother Goddess, who loves him dearly. She will not see him walk to his death. Rafe protects her children here, in her womb.'' Inca gestured toward the jungle nearby.

''This is a lot more dangerous than he's letting on, isn't it?''

Shrugging negligently, Inca rested her hands on her narrow hips. ''What is danger? A child reaching for a hot kettle suspended over a fire? A man falling in love with a forbidden woman? Going to track a kidnapped child? Humph. There is more danger in the man loving the woman than in any search for a kidnapped child, believe me.''

Stymied by her mysterious response, Ari stood there and tried to understand Inca's words. A man loving a forbidden woman. What was she talking about? How could love be forbidden?

Inca sighed and went to the blackened coffeepot at the edge of the dying fire. Handling it deftly, she grabbed a clean mug that sat near one of the logs. Pouring the thick, fragrant black coffee, she glanced up at Ari. ''You are *norteamericana*. He, *sulamericano*. Is that not forbidden?''

The words crawled through Ari as she watched Inca straighten and sip the coffee, her willow-green

gaze narrowed on the muddy Amazon River in front
of them. She stood with one hand on her hip, one
booted foot lifted up and resting on the log. Even
when she was slouched and seemingly at ease, there
was nothing relaxed about Inca. She was like an animal, constantly alert, with a fine tension sizzling
around her.

"Well?"

Inca's voice snapped through her. Fighting the in-
timidation she felt around the woman warrior, Ari
asked, "Why can't people from North and South
America get along?"

Chuckling, Inca sipped more of the coffee. "Why
not, indeed?" She lowered the cup, the smile disappearing from her oval face. Her eyes turned darker
green as she held Ari's gaze. "Only courage can see
the two nations meet and melt into one. You must
find that courage here. Now."

Stymied again by Inca's statements, Ari watched
as Rafe emerged from below, a knapsack over one
shoulder and a rifle in his right hand. A frisson of
fear shot through her.

"He will be safe," Inca assured her calmly. "Do
not blow things out of proportion, Ari."

Ari felt no sense of safety. Still, when she walked
to meet Rafe as he put his gear into the small aluminum, motorized skiff, Inca's words swirled in her
head. Ari had heard so much about the infamous
jaguar goddess. She didn't seem like a murderer to
Ari. Just the opposite. Inca seemed like someone
who cared deeply about all things—even Ari as she

panicked over possibly losing Rafe to a bullet from a drug runner and kidnapper.

"Take care of yourself?" Ari called as Rafe stepped into the boat.

He smiled slightly for her benefit. "For you, *mi flor,* I will."

Ari bit back the rest of her feelings. Rafe's kiss still tingled madly on her compressed lips. She folded her arms against her chest, feeling vulnerable. "I'll miss you, Rafe—our talks, making breakfast...."

As he pushed the skiff away from the bank of the channel, he sat down at the stern. "Even washing and drying dishes?" He teased.

Ari laughed a little and stepped closer. He reached toward the motor and pulled a cord. The little engine chattered to life, a cloud of bluish smoke rising in the wake. "Yes, even that."

Lifting his hand, Rafe called, "I'll see you in my dreams...."

Somehow, Ari thought, as she watched Rafe steer the skiff out of the channel and downriver, he always knew the right words to say to her.

Inca came and stood next to her. "Little sister, you and I are going to be very busy the week he is gone." She slanted her an amused glance. "You will not have time to worry about him. You will only have time to worry about yourself," she declared, and laughed deeply, the sound soothing Ari's troubled heart as she watched Rafe's boat disappear in the distance.

Chapter Seven

True to her word Inca kept Ari very busy for the next week, taking her on guided tours of the jungle to search for orchids. Now, as Ari stood looking up at a thirty-foot waterfall Inca had led her to, she gasped with delight. There among the mosses and ferns she could see a deep pink and crimson Cattleya orchid. She couldn't determine which type, because it hung on a grayish-colored dead limb that extended out over the water, which sprayed in an arc to the oblong pool below.

"It's beautiful!" she whispered excitedly to Inca, who stood at her shoulder. Looking around, Ari added, "What a wonderful place. It feels so peaceful here."

Inca grinned knowingly and studied the orchid

halfway up the rocky incline beside the waterfall. "This is one of my favorite places to rest and sleep. It is safe here."

They had hiked five miles into the jungle to find the specimen. Now, as Ari shrugged out of her knapsack, she realized she faced an even greater obstacle. "I don't know how I can draw the orchid up there, Inca. I'm afraid of heights."

Giving her a glance, Inca shrugged. "So? Climb up there and sit on that black rock near the dead limb. It is a perfect place to draw the orchid from. The spray from the waterfall will not reach you there, yet you will be close enough to study the orchid fully."

A squiggle of fear threaded through Ari's stomach. All week long Inca had shepherded her along, and each day posing a new challenge to her in some way. The fearless woman warrior seemed to pick out situations where Ari had to confront her fears. And each day, Inca had been there to cajole her and support her as Ari stepped out of her routine way of life and walked through her fears. Ari couldn't complain, because Inca had been showing her orchids of incredible color that weren't in any of her orchid identification books—orchids that were undiscovered—until now. As she drew and took photos of them, Ari knew that when she sent documentation to the orchid society to register them, the world would gasp in awe at their beauty. Not only that, but if the orchids were truly undiscovered until now, she would be able to name one after her mother, something Ari wanted to do more than anything. And in honor of Inca, she would name one of them after her as well.

"If you want to draw that orchid," Inca told her, as she pointed up at it, "then you must conquer your fear of heights, Ari."

Standing there, Ari felt another frisson of anxiety. "It's my greatest fear," she muttered.

Inca threw back her head and laughed. Then, placing her rifle against a tree, she turned and held Ari's gaze. "Do not defer to your weakness, little sister. You are a woman. Women are naturally strong. Stronger than any male of any species." She walked over, picked up Ari's knapsack and opened it. Taking out the box of colored pencils and the sketchbook, she said, "You were raised to cower in front of men. To be a true woman, you must embrace your own powers, fears and all, and do what you must do. That orchid has been seen only by my eyes and those of the insects and animals. You said you wanted to name an orchid after your mother. What better way to honor her than with this one, eh?" Inca peered into Ari's face. "Well?"

Gulping, Ari felt the power of Inca. Her willow-green eyes were narrowed and thoughtful. All week Inca had taught her to make fear her friend, let it walk beside her—but not stop her.

"W-what if I fall?"

Inca straightened and smiled mirthlessly. "Then you will pick yourself back up, dust off your muddy pants and try again. Do you think life accepts quitters? No. Life only honors those who are strong.

Those who can endure and keep going. So, what will you do with this day, little sister? Will you pine and whine down here, at the foot of the hill? Or will you take the challenge and meet it the best way you can? There is no dishonor in failing. There is dishonor in not trying at all." A bit of scorn laced her husky voice. "In my realm, a woman or man who does not try does not live." She touched the front of Ari's pale pink blouse. "What does your heart say to do?"

"Get up there and draw that orchid." Ari replied, studying her companion's playful expression. Inca's attitude right now belied the military garb she wore. Every day she was armed and alert. And although she never said they were in danger as they made their five and ten mile hikes through the jungle, Ari sometimes felt that they might be. Still, being in Inca's powerful presence, she rarely felt unprotected.

"And what is your head screaming at you to do?" Inca's mouth curved.

Ari sighed. "You know without asking me. I'm scared."

"What is it shrieking at you?"

"That I can't do it. That heights make me dizzy...."

"And where did this fear come from?"

"I don't know."

"Yes, you do."

Stymied, Ari frowned at Inca. Rafe would say nearly the same words to her. Was it an Indian thing? A South American way of looking at life's obstacles? Thinking back, she murmured, "My mother was afraid of heights."

"And did you see her being afraid of them?"

"Yes, many times."

"And so, as a child, you took on her fear. Before that, you were like the monkeys that climb effortlessly up the trunks of trees and swing limb to limb."

Ari stood there, looking at the sunlight that sometimes peeked through the canopy to touch the spray of water. When it did, she would see a brief bit of a rainbow arc halfway down the waterfall to the pond, below where they stood.

"Sometimes I think you read my mind," Ari accused her petulantly. "Yes, I remember when I was six my mother had to climb up on a ladder to rescue me from a tree I'd climbed. I remember her face. It was so white. She was so shaky and unsteady on that ladder."

"But *she* conquered her fear to come and rescue you, did she not?"

Ari saw Inca's carefully drawn point and grinned up at her companion. "You missed your calling, Inca. You should have been a teacher."

A pleased smile tugged at Inca's wide mouth. "We are all teachers to one another, little sister. So, go climb and paint your orchid for your mother."

It wasn't easy for Ari, despite Inca's support. Still, she took the items from Inca, placed them back into the knapsack then shrugged the bag across her shoulders and slowly moved to the right side of the pool. She marveled once more at what an incredibly beautiful place this was, with many huge, gray-trunked trees supported by root systems that looked like flying buttresses. There were shiny-leafed coffee bushes here and there, and ferns grew luxuriantly along both sides of the falls, nourished and humidified by the spray of water.

Ari's heart was beating hard in her chest. Fear ate at her. Looking around for the best path up through the curving ferns, she hesitated as she spied black rocks jutting out here and there, most of them covered in a springy, yellowish-green moss.

She heard Inca's low, growling tone right behind her, as if she were leaning over and whispering in her ear. "Life rewards those who take the risks. Do you want to see yourself as a quitter? As someone who refuses to meet the challenge?"

Jerking around, she saw that Inca was a good twenty feet away. Rubbing her temple, Ari wondered at the closeness of Inca's voice. The woman warrior was sitting up against one of the buttress roots, field stripping her rifle on a clean white cloth, a small can of oil nearby.

Confused, Ari turned and looked up the side of the falls. It was only fifteen feet high, but to her, it looked a thousand. There was a serviceable path up the side of it where the Cattleya orchid lived on the outstretched branch. It looked safe enough. She put her booted foot on the first rock and pushed to test it. It held firmly. Already she felt perspiration dotting her lip and forehead. Her heart wouldn't stop hammering in her chest. Chewing on her lip, Ari asked herself why she was here in the first place. Okay, so her mother had had a fear of heights. Inca was suggesting Ari didn't. Flexing her hands nervously, Ari stretched up and gripped the next moss-covered rock above her. Testing it, she discovered the rock was solid.

"Good, little sister. One step at a time. That is how fear is overcome. Tell it that you know it is there. That you invite it to come along with you, but that you will not allow it to stop you from reaching out for your dream...."

Inca's voice sounded inside her head. Turning, Ari saw the woman warrior hadn't moved from her spot, her head bent over the rifle as she oiled the metal mechanisms.

"Come on, Ari! You can't be a coward down here in South America!" she told herself fiercely. Inca was right: she had to do this for her mother. She *wanted* that orchid for her growing collection of illustrations. In that instant, Ari felt a vague shift deep within her. It wasn't anything she could pinpoint exactly, only that it seemed to her like a car shifting gears. The fear in her, the edginess, lessened in intensity. Lifting her head, Ari resolutely stretched her other hand upward to grip the next rock. She began the climb.

Knees a little weak after she had found a perch to sit on directly in front of the luscious-looking Cattleya orchid, Ari cautiously looked around. She was fifteen feet above the ground. She gripped the knapsack hard after she carefully shrugged out of it. The roar of the water was musical to her. She sat well enough away from the spray to keep dry. The orchid was five feet away, suspended out over the water on the dead limb.

Forcing herself to look down, she saw Inca was still working on her rifle, paying absolutely no attention to her. If Inca had been worried, Ari was sure she'd be watching her. More of her fear dissolved. She'd made it. She was up here. A thread of joy surged through her. She heard Inca's husky laughter inside her head.

"You see, little sister? That fear is your companion, but once he knows you are going to step out and live your life, he slinks away like the coward he really is."

Ari wondered once again at Inca's guiding voice. Rafe had warned her that his friend was mysterious. He had hinted that she could read minds and could "talk" with mental telepathy. As Ari drew out her sketchbook and colored pencils, she smiled gamely. Inca was with her in spirit; Ari could sense it. She could feel the woman's presence around her like a soft, protective blanket. Or was it her vivid imagination once more? Shaking her head, Ari wasn't sure. Concentrating on the orchid instead, she began to draw quickly and confidently. No longer did it take her a week to finish one drawing. No, since Inca had come, they would trek into the heart of the jungle each morning. By midday, Inca would find an orchid for her, and Ari would spend the afternoon capturing it on paper. Toward early evening, they would walk back to camp, and by nightfall be enjoying a well-earned meal around the warmth and light of the campfire.

As Ari drew now, her strokes with the colored pencils were confident, even bold. She became lost in the vivid colors of the Cattleya orchid. The flower had five oblong petals, two to three inches in length. The outer lip of the orchid was a crimson color, the inner lip a deep gold. The leather, oval-shaped leaves thrust up around the single blossom, emphasizing the brilliant colors of the flower.

As she continued to draw, Ari's thoughts turned to Rafe. When would he get home? Every day she worried about his safety. Inca would laugh at her, pat her on the shoulder and tell her that he was fine. For whatever reason, Ari believed the woman. There was something about Inca's knowing that left no room for questioning. Besides, Ari had seen for herself how the people of Aroka's village idolized Inca. She had gone with Inca on one of her trips to the village and watched as the woman warrior lay her hands on the sick and ailing. Ari was amazed at how Inca's touch could make a baby or elderly person well. She knew she was seeing healing because it was impossible for a baby to fake sickness. And as for the older people of Aroka's village who limped painfully around using a gnarled wood cane for support, they would throw their canes away after Inca had smoothed her long, beautifully slender hands across the injured or swollen extremity.

The orchid bloomed across the page of Ari's

sketchbook. Today the drawing was going excep-
tionally well and twice as fast. Ari looked up from
her work and saw Inca down below reassembling her
rifle. Every day the woman cleaned her equipment.
In this humidity, rust was a real problem, Ari had
been told. Ari knew little about guns or weapons of
war, but Inca's knowledge of warfare had shown her
that a woman could be anything. One moment Inca
was a healer nursing the sick, another, a warrior in
full armament. Inca's compassion was renowned, according to Aroka's wife. The villagers of Amazonia
always looked forward to her visiting them. The old,
infirm and sick would line up and wait patiently as
she placed her hands on each of them.

No wonder Rafe thought so much of Inca. Ari
smiled softly and returned to her drawing. The orchid
seemed to leap off the page, vividly alive beneath
her hands. Was it because she felt incredibly happy
whenever Rafe came to mind? Missing him acutely,
Ari longed to see his handsome, smiling features—
especially those dark brown eyes that sparkled with
a smoldering heat whenever he looked at her.

Inca had said he would be back by tonight. Would
he? Her pulse raced a little at that possibility. She
missed his laughter, his insightfulness about life and
about her. Ari felt a powerful, sweeping emotion
rock her heart. Could this be love she felt for Rafe?
They barely knew each other. Her mother had said
that real love lasted through time and could not be
made on the spur of the moment. Ari decided that
when her drawing was done and she climbed down

from her perch, she'd ask Inca about love. Surely, as beautiful as Inca was, she would know more about it than Ari did.

"Congratulations," Inca said as Ari sat down with her near the tree with the buttress roots. "You did it."

Smiling widely, Ari reached out and touched Inca's firm arm. "Thanks to you."

"Oh, no," Inca chortled, "you did it all on your own." Her eyes glimmered with merriment. "When Rafe returns tonight, he will meet a new woman. The old one he left has died. A new one has been born. I think he will be very pleased." Inca spread out their lunch before them. "More importantly, you must be pleased with how you are growing. You are like a young sapling denied sunlight for too long, but now that you have experienced it, you are changing daily, growing into the great tree you will eventually become."

Ari settled opposite her, her legs crossed. "I feel different. Better." Then she laughed and flexed her arm so that her biceps showed. "And I am getting stronger because of you and these hikes!"

Above them, the sunlight filtered through the canopy. Tiny squirrel monkeys with white masks across their eyes chirped and hopped nearby, hoping for a morsel. A kapok tree, which had white flowers and fruit in scarlet pods, hung nearby. The rain forest was a feast of color and music from birds, monkeys and insects.

Inca handed her a beef sandwich with mayonnaise. "You do not see the other changes?" She munched on a ripe mango. Scattered around her were hulled Brazil nuts, thick and oblong in shape.

Ari bobbed her head as she ate with gusto. "Sure I do. I'm happier than I've ever been. I feel strong here." She pointed to her stomach. "I'm not the sniveling shadow of before." She laughed self-consciously. "I *know* Rafe and you probably thought I was the biggest mouse you'd ever seen. I used to be afraid of my own shadow."

With a tilt of her head, Inca smiled, showing her strong white teeth. "And now, jaguar cub? You have felt your own power, have you not? It is a good feeling, eh?"

"It's nice," Ari admitted. "I scare myself sometimes with the feelings inside of me, Inca. I owe a lot to you. I noticed that every day you give me challenges that are a little tougher to surmount than the day before."

"And you conquer them," Inca said in praise. "Do you not think I am also afraid? I am. But the difference is I do not allow it to stop me. No one and nothing has the right to stop you on your own path as you become all you can be, Ari."

Peeling another mango, Ari suddenly sobered. "Yes, I'm beginning to understand what you're saying, Inca. Before it was just words. Now I'm *feeling it.*"

"That is the difference." Inca regarded her as she reached for a handful of the nuts on the cloth.

"When a woman feels her power for the first time, it feels strange and awkward to her. Later she will grow accustomed to it, and then she will feel the real power of herself. *That* is how all women should feel, but in this world, they do not. I am saddened by it. But you have the heart and the courage to reach out. Rafe was right about you—you are courageous and only needed a little watering and sunlight to help you grow into your full self."

Chuckling, Ari finished off her sandwich. Inca handed her some nuts and she took them with thanks. She threw one of them to a monkey that sat up on his haunches nearby, then watched him skitter off with his newly found treasure.

"Well, I'm trying," she told Inca. "By the time I get back to Washington, my father and friends won't know me."

"Hmm." Wiping her mouth with the back of her hand, Inca reached for a canteen of water from the webbed belt around her waist. "More important is that you like what you are becoming. What they think does not matter."

"Ouch...that's a big one to overcome. I always worry what others think of me."

Barking with laughter, Inca said, "If I worried what everyone thought of me, I would have been dead a long time ago." She tipped up the canteen, the gleam of her throat visible as she drank deeply. Placing the cap back on the canteen, Inca gave Ari an amused look. "People's opinions do not— cannot—count. What you must do is ask your heart how you feel about yourself. There is truth in our hearts. Always. If someone calls me a murderer, do I believe them? No, because I know the truth of the situation. You must trust your heart, little sister, at all times, without turning away from it and letting the head chatter make decisions for you instead.''

Ari sighed. She felt stuffed. Opening a bottle of water, she drank a little. ''Inca, I have a question for you.''

''Yes?''

With a twist of her lips, Ari said, ''About love. I feel all these strange, new and wonderful feelings for Rafe. I've never felt them before and I'm not sure what it is. What they are.'' She gave Inca a searching look as she packed away the wrappings from the sandwich into her knapsack. ''Have you been in love? Do you know what it feels like?''

Inca blew a strand of her dark hair off her brow. She leaned back, her arms hanging languidly over her drawn-up knees as she made herself comfortable against the thick, gray wing of the root. ''Love? That is one thing I have never felt. At least, not yet.''

''But you're my age.''

''Have you fallen in love yet?'' Inca demanded testily.

''Well…no, but…''

''What? You expect I have and should be able to tell you about it?'' Her mouth lifted. ''Do I know what love *feels* like? I know I feel deeply for those who come under my care, for what I can give them from the Great Mother Goddess. I have many emo-

tions for different things in my life—the love I feel
when I cradle a baby in my arms, the love for a
young child who is crying and in pain...or for a
woman who is in labor and who needs my care and
nurturing.''

"I see your point," Ari murmured sympatheti-
cally. "You just seem so worldly, Inca. So confident
and strong. I thought that some man would idolize
the ground you walked on, would love you as
fiercely as you love life. I've never seen anyone like
you before. You're able to reach out, grab every minute, live every hour to its fullest. I see the emotions
on your face. I hear them in your voice. I feel them
when you touch something. You're so in tune with
everything...."

"Just because I am does not mean I know what
love between a man and a woman is."

Somberly, Ari wrapped up the cloth that had
served as their makeshift table. "But you're so beautiful...."

Harsh laughter filled the air. "Me? Beautiful? Little sister, do not be fooled by how someone looks
on the outside. Be far more concerned about what is
here." She tapped her heart. "Besides, no man
would have me. I'm too fierce. Too much my own
person. Men cower in front of me. They run. They
are frightened of me, of my power. I have yet to
meet a man, with the exception of Rafe and Michael
Houston, my other brother in Amazonia, who can
stand to be with me for long." Shaking her head,

Inca said, "No, I am destined to live my life alone. I came in alone. I will die alone."

Frowning, Ari said, "I feel you're wrong. Surely if Rafe accepts you and isn't threatened by you, who you are, there's got to be some man who will admire and respect you for who you are?"

"My blood brother, Michael Houston, does as does Rafe," Inca said more to herself as she gazed up through the jungle roof. "There are two men who are not afraid of me, who can stand being in my presence without wanting to tear me down or destroy me." She tipped her head so that she could look at Ari. "When a woman becomes self-empowered, most men want to destroy her. For too long they have kept women crushed beneath their masculine energy with threats of harming or killing them. I see it to this day. Here in Brazil a wife can be shot by her husband if he thinks she even *looks* at another man. And yet the husband can have a mistress and boast about it, and the wife can do nothing."

Grimly, Inca sat up, her voice dropping to a growl. "There are many injustices against we who live in a woman's form. That is wrong. I do what I can to right it here, in Amazonia, where I live. But I am only one person. What must happen is that each woman must embrace her own power herself. And then she must stand the tests and not allow it to ever be stripped from her again."

"I hear you," Ari murmured. "I see it all the time where I live, as well. Women aren't paid as much as a man for the same job. They don't get the same opportunities, either. There's a lot of spousal abuse that goes on, too.''

"Well," Inca said, "I cannot tell you much about a man falling in love with you, little sister, but it is clear to me that you are empowering yourself so you need not worry about it. As for me, my life is here." She gestured to the jungle surrounding them. "My destiny is here. I was born here, they say, on a stormy night during the eclipse of the moon. I was born in total darkness except for the dance of lightning and the drumming of thunder to welcome me into this world. I have storm medicine, and I walk with the Jaguar Clan. My destiny is to protect my people, the Indians, from white men who would rape, kill and enslave them. No, there is no man who has the guts, the heart, to love me, so that is why I cannot tell you about it."

Saddened, Ari glanced at Inca, whose expression revealed an incredible loneliness. "I hope you're wrong, Inca. You deserve a man who is as strong and brave and committed as you are."

"Well, if he exists, it is only in my imagination." She laughed sharply. "But what of these feelings you have for Rafe?"

Opening her hands, Ari muttered, "Inca, I don't know if it's possible to fall in love in such a short time. My mother said only time would show if love was true and lasting."

"Wise words from your mother."

"Whenever he looks at me, my heart swells." Ari pressed her hand against her chest. "I feel like I can't take in a breath of air—I'm under his spell. He has the most wonderful eyes. I used to avoid looking at people's eyes, but not his. I find myself wanting to look at him, to eat him up with my gaze.'' She laughed self-consciously. ''I almost ache to feel him touch me lightly with his fingers. Oh, it's nothing serious—you know how he touches others. He's a toucher.''

''Yes, one of the many things about Rafe I admire,'' Inca murmured. ''Most men cannot reach out and touch, console or embrace others when they are hurting. He can. So can my other brother, Michael Houston. He is good to his wife, Anne, and his baby.''

Nodding, Ari leaned forward, legs crossed, hands open toward Inca. ''Well, then you do understand. I've had boyfriends when I was going to university, but the feelings I felt for them were nothing compared to what I feel for Rafe! When he kissed me, before he left, I felt my whole world rock. My knees became jelly, Inca. They've never done that before! And I so look forward to the evenings with him, when we work in the galley together. I love his teasing, his laughter that's so rich and deep....''

''I think you are meant for him,'' Inca said seriously. ''I have never seen Rafe as happy as when I walked into camp a week ago. There is new light in his eyes. He smiles often. And the way he looks at you when you do not know it is that of a jaguar finding his mate.''

"Really?" Her heart bounded once to underscore Inca's softly spoken words.

"Rafe has a deeply wounded heart, little sister. Has he told you of his father disowning him? Writing him out of the will? Denying that he even exists? And then Justine, the woman he fell in love with, spurned him because he refused to leave his home here in the rain forest. Rafe carries deep grief within him over these things. He also believes that he, like me, will never find someone who will share his love of Amazonia, of the things that matter to him. He and I have spoken often of this. What woman would want this kind of life? He is often gone from his camp. He is in danger sometimes. He is the first to arrive at a village when it faces an epidemic, so he risks his life in that way, too. When there is a natural disaster, when the great Amazon floods and people are marooned, he must find and rescue them. When the fierce storm god comes over and sends water pouring down upon us for days on end, people need his help, the food he can find, to keep them alive. What woman would want a man like that?"

Ari almost blurted, "I would," but bit her lower lip instead. "Rafe is committed to his dream. To what he does best."

"Rafe and I run on our hearts, our passions. We do *only* what we love, Ari. Nothing more. Nothing less." She gestured lazily toward her. "You need to find out what your passion is. And if it matches and mates with Rafe's, then perhaps you have what it will take to love him and accept him as he is. If you cannot, then you should go home when you are done here. Rafe is not a man who gives his heart easily. I know of only one time since I have known him that he fell in love, and it was with Justine, a very rich and powerful woman. She was a psychologist in Manaus who tried coming out here. But the lure of the city was too much for her. Rafe had hoped she would fall in love with the Amazon as he had.'' Shaking her head, Inca muttered, ''It was not to be. I could see it coming, but there was nothing I could do or say to stop him from making the choices he made. He is in command of his own life, not I.''

''How sad,'' Ari murmured. ''Rafe deserves a woman. A friend. A companion for life out here.'' She gazed around the area. ''How anyone could *not* fall in love with this place is beyond me. Every day there is something new to look at, to smell, to touch. The colors here are never the same two days in a row. There is such life here, Inca.''

Inca regarded her from half-closed eyes. ''So, perhaps you need to look at your life differently? Perhaps home is not where you believe it to be? When you get your drawings done, you will leave us. The real question is will you return? Rafe needs a woman who wants to live here.'' She jabbed her finger toward the dark brown, rotting leaves that littered the ground. ''Find the roots of your real home in your heart, little sister. Then you will have the answer.''

Ari nodded. ''Now I'm more confused than ever.''

Inca stretched to her full height. ''Life is really simple if you allow it to be. Let the mud of your confusion settle on the bottom, then the clarity of the water above will be seen. Come, we must begin our trek back to camp. I feel Rafe is going to beat us home if we do not hurry.''

Excited by the possibility of seeing Rafe once again, Ari clambered to her feet and rapidly shrugged on her day pack. Grinning, she said, ''Let's go!''

Chapter Eight

"Rafe!" Ari called when she saw him guiding the aluminum skiff near the bank of the Amazon, her voice echoing excitedly through the campsite.

She ran to where he eased the bow of the boat into the channel. He smiled at her tiredly, his unshaved face bristly with about a week's worth of growth.

"Here," he called, "tie the line up to that tree?" He tossed her the cotton rope that would hold the bow firmly to the bank.

"Sure," Ari called, happiness in her voice as she caught the line and tied it around a stump on the bank. As she straightened she noted that he looked exceedingly tired. There were dark circles beneath his eyes and she sensed great sadness around him as he eased out of the skiff. As he leaped to the bank and moved toward her, Ari saw grief in his dark brown eyes.

"I missed you so much!" she cried, spontaneously throwing her arms around his neck and pressing herself against him.

Rafe halted, surprised at her gesture. Within seconds, he was embracing her tightly against him. How good her soft, firm body felt next to his. He was a thief, stealing comfort from her warm, lithe form for just a moment. Her arms barely reached around his neck, such was the difference in their heights. When she turned her face toward him and kissed his cheek, he groaned.

"I stink, Ari. I haven't had a shower or shaved in seven days." Justine had always recoiled from him when he wasn't clean. Despite the fact that living in the rain forest made sweat and dirt part of his everyday life, Justine had hated it.

Laughing giddily, the feel of his arms wonderful to her, Ari whispered breathlessly, "I don't care, Rafe. You're here. You're safe. That's all I care about...."

How badly he wanted to kiss her, but he knew that Ari was not his to take or to keep. She was transient in his life, a sunbeam that would leave him someday. Wrapping his hands around her waist, he eased her away. "You look beautiful to me," he said huskily. Her eyes were alive with joy, with sunlight dancing in the light blue depths. Her cheeks were flushed like ripe berries. Most of all, he ached to meet and touch that soft, smiling mouth of hers. He hadn't forgotten their kiss. Throughout the miserable week, he'd replayed that kiss a hundred times, especially when his journey had come to a sad end. Ari represented life and joy to him, there was no doubt.

Rafe forced himself to reluctantly release her and climb the bank. By the fire, he saw Inca standing, her arms across her breasts, watching him through half-closed glittering green eyes. He felt the touch of her mind upon his; by now he was used to her ability to communicate telepathically. He wondered if Inca had fully revealed herself to Ari this week. One corner of Inca's mouth pulled upward and she gave him a wry look, shaking her head in response to his unspoken question.

Ari wrapped her arm around Rafe's waist and guided him toward the campfire. "Inca and I have a pot of beans, some freshly made white rice and some beef for you. You must be starved." She poked at his rib cage. "Have you lost weight? You look like you have." His cheeks were more hollow than Ari recalled and she couldn't help but notice that Rafe was right, he stank. His clothes were dirty, smudged and ground in with dirt and days of unrelenting sweat. His boots were caked with dried red mud, as were the bottoms of his khaki trousers. She saw his mouth lift tiredly at her gentle teasing.

"Food. I'm ready for some. Eating on the run isn't exactly hotel fare."

"Sit down," Ari said excitedly, "and I'll dish it

up for you. Inca, will you pour him some of the coffee, please?''

Rafe looked obliquely over at Inca, who took a seat on a stump opposite them. She was grinning like a jaguar who had sited her quarry. Giving her a quizzical look, he nodded his thanks as Ari handed him a plate of steaming beans, rice and beef, a customary dish in Brazil, and one he'd been raised on. Right now, he was famished for it. Placing the plate on his lap, he dug into the fare with his fork.

Inca handed him a tin cup filled with hot, fresh coffee.

''Thanks,'' he mumbled between bites.

Ari sat down next to him and took a good look at him. Rafe desperately needed to shower and shave. He looked darkly dangerous with that growth of beard on his face. What bothered her was the look in his eyes. They were a flat brown color, and she sensed grief around him. She bit her tongue, because she wanted to wait until he'd eaten before she asked him about his adventures downriver.

Rafe glanced up at Ari, who sat a good three feet away from him, her hands curled around one of her upraised knees. ''How did your week go, *mi flor?*''

Inca shared a smile with Rafe. *''Mi flor?''* she teased.

Taking a slab of bread from Ari, who had thoughtfully buttered it for him, he grinned rakishly. ''She reminds me of a flower.''

''Well,'' Inca drawled, ''your flower bloomed this

past week. You will be proud of her. She has unfolded many of her petals in your absence.''

Ari felt heat stinging her cheeks. ''Oh, Inca...''

Inca's thick, arched brows rose. ''Have I not spoken the truth? Why do you not tell Rafe of all that you have accomplished?'' She jabbed a finger at the sketchbook that sat near Ari. ''And that you have seven more orchid drawings than before he left?''

Rafe looked at Ari. ''Seven? That's great. A real improvement.'' Right now, he wanted to hear good news. He saw her smile in response.

''Inca is trying to get me to embrace my own power.''

''It's working.''

Ari shrugged, painfully self-conscious beneath his warming inspection. ''Well...I'm trying, and you said that's all that counts, right?''

Inca grinned and shifted her attention to Rafe. ''I must get going, my brother. You are in the capable hands of a young jaguar woman in training, here. I hope she will share all her adventures, of which there are many, with you as you eat.''

Inca rose and went over to slide the bandoleers over her head and pick up her web belt, which she methodically buckled around her waist. ''I will be around if you need me again,'' she called to them, and lifted her hand.

Ari raised her hand. ''Do you *have* to leave, Inca?'' She saw the woman lean over and pick up her rifle, which was never far from her hand.

Straightening, Inca laughed. "Are you not tired of confronting all your fears daily with me around?"

Ari stood and went over to her. The dusk was deepening around them, the sky an apricot hue. The shadows emphasized Inca's strong, caring features. "How can I ever repay you?"

Sliding the leather sling of the rifle across her left shoulder, the butt of the rifle up so that rain would not leak down into the barrel and rust it, she eyed Rafe, who was watching them as he ate. "Take care of him, little sister," she told her in a whisper. Inca touched her arm. "He is grieving. Things did not go well for him down in the other village. He needs you. Be there for him?"

Shaken by the growl in Inca's lowered tone, Ari said, "Of course I will."

"Good." Inca stepped away from her. She raised her hand in Rafe's direction. "I will be near if you call."

"Thanks, Inca…" he said wearily, and lifted his hand in farewell. "Thanks for taking care of Ari while I was gone."

Inca laughed. It was more a roughened purr. "She is *not* the same shadow you left behind, my brother. This is a woman who is learning to be a jaguar."

Rafe grinned tiredly. "I was hoping you'd show her the ropes."

Ari said goodbye to Inca, who turned, trotted down the path toward the Juma village, and was quickly swallowed up by the jungle. Turning, Ari sighed and walked back to the campfire. Rafe followed her progress, and she saw that smoldering look that always lingered in his eyes when he stared at her. It made her feel good and strong about herself as a woman. As a person. Sitting down near him, she picked up her sketchbook and automatically placed it in her lap.

"You look tired, Rafe. Is there anything I can do for you?"

"Nothing that a hot shower and about twelve hours of sleep won't fix," he told her. Using the last of the bread, he wiped the bottom of his plate.

Nodding, Ari remembered Inca's warning that things hadn't gone well for Rafe at the village. Her stomach knotted in anticipation of possible bad news.

"I wonder how Inca can know something without hearing it," she said, mystified. "She told me you'd be coming home at dusk today, so we left the waterfall a little early to get back here to make a pot of fresh beans for your arrival."

Rafe set the tin plate aside and picked up his coffee, holding it in both his hands. If he didn't, he was going to slide his one hand around Ari's shoulders and draw her to him. He ached to hold her. He *needed* to hold her. She couldn't know. Not ever. "Inca is a member of the Jaguar Clan, Ari. The members of the clan are clairvoyant."

"Humph," Ari said, "I think she can read my mind, too."

Grinning slightly as he lifted the cup, Rafe said, "Oh, she's well known for that."

"Sometimes she'd say something about what I was thinking about or mulling over in my mind. She'd pop up with a response when I hadn't even asked my question out loud yet."

"Did you get used to her ways as the week wore on?" he asked with a grin.

Laughing, Ari said, "Yes. She's a wonderful person, Rafe. She taught me so much!"

"I can see that," he murmured, pleased. "You appear much more sure of yourself. And I see when you walk, your shoulders are thrown back with pride."

Wrinkling her nose, she murmured, "Oh, that. Inca was on me mercilessly to hold my chin up, walk with my shoulders back. She was like a drill sergeant all week about my posture."

Chuckling pleasantly, Rafe drained the rest of his coffee and set the cup down by his boots. "If Inca cares about you, you get on the receiving end of her 'tough love.' If she didn't care about you, she wouldn't say a thing."

"She taught me so much, Rafe." Ari opened her hands, excitement in her voice. "I know you're tired, so I don't want to avalanche you with all that happened. I think you need to take a hot shower now and go to sleep. Why don't you use my bed? I'll just curl up out here in your hammock."

Grateful for her care and sensitivity, he said, "You know what I would like?" He reached out and briefly touched her hand.

"No. What?"

"Let me make up that second bed across the aisle from you. It's supposed to rain tonight." He looked up at the sky, which was becoming inky as the blue and purple shadows of night rapidly skimmed across it. He saw flashes of lightning in the distance. "And I need to get some sleep to bounce back from the hell of the last seven days."

Ari watched the lightning dance across the sky to the west of them. Although it was the dry season, sometimes a thunderstorm would crop up unexpectedly, producing a half-hour downpour. It had happened once while Inca was with her, and she had slept across the aisle from her in the houseboat.

"Of course, it's your boat. I'm just a guest."

Rafe wanted her to be so much more to him. This last week had hammered home how lonely he was without Ari's sunlit presence in his life. It had burdened his grief-stricken heart even more. "You're never a guest, *mi flor*. You're a part of this rain forest." And then he added silently *and a part of me*. He bit back the rest of what he was going to say.

Touched beyond words, Ari reached over and squeezed his hand. "Let me go get you a fresh towel and cloth. While you're showering, I'll make up your bed for you. You look like you're ready to keel over."

Grateful, his hand tingling where she'd grazed it with her fingertips, he could only nod. A well of grief, of emotion, rose like a huge, pressurized ball in the center of his chest. He swallowed hard. Swallowed against the need to weep. Ari brought out all his emotions, and he was nearly helpless to stop them.

As she rose and quickly moved toward the houseboat, he reached over and poured himself another cup of coffee. He wanted something stronger. A helluva lot stronger. As exhausted as he was, he wanted nothing more than to pull Ari into his bed, hold her in his arms and sob. He knew she could be strong for him when he was weak. And right now, he was at low ebb. Usually when things such as this happened he was alone at his camp. He could go out on the bow of his boat, deep in the night, and sob out the pain he carried. What was he going to do now? His heart ached to have Ari in his arms, to tell her the terrible story he held inside, to ease the burden of sadness.

Sternly, Rafe told himself that could never be. To be that intimate with Ari was to take advantage of her good nature. She was a woman who was here for a short amount of time, and then she would return to her world and leave him behind. For him to share so much with her was a form of commitment to her and he didn't dare trip that lever open. No, somehow—for her sake—he must try and grapple with the pressure within his chest, the wildly clamoring emotions that pleaded to be released differently this time.

Ari awoke with a jerk. What was that sound? Sitting up, the light sheet falling away and exposing the pale lavender, cotton nightgown she wore, she quickly looked around. A sound had awakened her from her deep sleep. Thunder rumbled nearby. One storm had already passed shortly before they had gone to bed in the hold of the houseboat. Now slivers of moonlight filtered in through the windows. The sluggish, humid air stirred, cooling the interior of the boat.

Looking across the aisle, Ari pushed several strands of hair away from her face. Rafe lay sprawled on his back, his pale blue pajamas twisted and the sheet tangled about his feet from his tossing and turning. In the moonlight, his smoothly shaved face looked gaunt, the hollows under his high cheekbones pronounced. There was something terribly vulnerable about him lying there, his arms flung outward, his legs tangled in bedding, a lock of hair dipping across his furrowed, sweaty brow.

It was the look on Rafe's face that made Ari bite back a cry. His features were frozen in a grimace, as if he was captured within a terrible nightmare. His chest was rising and falling rapidly, his lips parted in a soundless cry. She saw his large hands open and close spasmodically, the tension in his body very real. A moan tore from him.

That was the noise that had dragged Ari from her sleep. It was a terrible sound, one of desperation and grief. She watched as Rafe turned on his side, and saw a trickle of perspiration course down his temple toward his tightened jaw. Ari felt helpless, unsure of what to do, but something in her heart drove her to her feet. She found herself sitting hesitantly on the edge of his bed, her hands reaching for his shoulder and arm to comfort him.

"Rafe?" she whispered urgently. "Rafe, wake up. You're having a nightmare...." She shook him gently.

Jerking awake, Rafe reared back, sleep torn from him. He blinked several times, orienting himself to the fact that he was here, in the houseboat, and not out on the trail chasing drug runners. He felt Ari's cool touch on the overheated flesh of his arm.

"Ari?" He looked around, confused. What was she doing here on his bed? Why was that look of worry etched in her wide, sleepy eyes? "What's wrong? Did you hear something?" he asked anxiously. Rafe had been attacked by drug runners before. And after what had happened on this last mission, he wouldn't be surprised if they were paying him a visit.

"It's you," Ari said apologetically. "You were crying out. Like you needed help. It woke me up. I came over to try and help you. Nothing's wrong, Rafe...everything's quiet around here except for the storm coming."

Raking his fingers through his hair, he sat up, leaning with relief against the bulkhead. "Good..."

"I'm sorry. Maybe I shouldn't have woken you."

Looking over at her, he realized how close she was, and how innocent she looked in the pale lavender gown with lace across the front. He forced a partial smile. "No, it's all right. I was having a nightmare...just reliving what happened. I'm the one who is sorry, *mi flor*.'' And he reached out because he needed to touch her, to feel her life connecting with his. As he slid his fingers along the line of her jaw, her lips parted. Ari's eyes closed, the blond lashes delicate against her smooth, warm skin. How beautiful she looked with her hair mussed and tangled around her face and shoulders.

"Lord help me," he muttered savagely, "but I need you, Ari. Just let me hold you for a moment? Please?" It was all he could do to stop himself from dragging her into his arms.

Stunned by his low growl, she eased forward, lifting her arms and sliding them around his broad shoulders. As she moved over, her hip and thigh meeting his, she felt him tense momentarily. Giving him a small smile, she said, "I won't bite, Rafe. Just let me hold you. I know I can do that much for you."

Exhaustion muddled his mind and silenced his doubts. Right now, coming out of the terror of his nightmare, remembering how close to death he'd nearly come himself this past week, he more than welcomed her boldness. This was the new Ari, he thought as she, with her diminutive body, wrapped her arms around him and held him as best she could with her womanly strength.

So much of him felt relief from her ministrations, the way she gently threaded her fingers through his damp hair and positioned his head against her shoulder. She was surprisingly strong as she held him. But then weren't women stronger than men in many surprising ways? Rubbing his cheek against her shoulder, which was naked except for the thin strap of her gown, he released a long, shaky breath. The driving urge to tell her what had happened overwhelmed him. With his cheek pressed against her shoulder, her arms around his torso, he slid his hands around her waist and closed his eyes.

"I feel like I'm still trapped in hell," he muttered hoarsely.

"Tell me about it," Ari urged softly. She felt him tremble once, violently, as the silence deepened. The fact that Rafe entrusted himself to her arms, to her, made her spirit soar with joy. She rocked him gently back and forth as she might a baby that needed comforting. Rafe needed her now as never before, she knew.

"It was hell," he managed to relate in a low, hoarse tone. "The little boy who was kidnapped by the Valentino Brothers...we went after him. Me, the chief of the village and the men of the family from which he was stolen. The trail was fresh. We trotted or ran where we could, to try and make up the distance. But all the time, the kidnappers evaded us. They knew we were hot on their trail." He inhaled the sweet jasmine scent that lingered on her flesh and it eased his tightening stomach. Relaxing his grip from around her waist, Rafe moved his hand up the length of her arm and cupped her shoulder. She was soft and firm and incredibly appealing to his hungry senses.

"Did you ever catch them?"

His hand stilled on her shoulder. "Yes...on the

third day. We knew we were getting close to one of the cocaine factories they have hidden down in some of the deepest valleys. We knew we were in a lot of danger—that the Valentinos' soldiers could intercept us and wipe us out in minutes flat. I had a hunch, and we played it. We left their trail and decided to head in at an angle to intercept them." He squeezed his eyes shut, forcing out the words. "The child tried to escape. We heard shots. Close. Very close. I knew what had happened when we went crashing into their midst. The boy, just twelve, lay twisting and screaming on the rain forest floor. A firefight broke out. Most of the chief's men were killed. I managed to drag the boy out of the line of fire and then we retreated and ran."

Ari shut her eyes and rested her head against his. "I'm so sorry, Rafe. Did he live?"

A tremor shook him. "The father of the boy was killed in the firefight. So was an uncle. I carried the boy. Blood was running down my arms, down my pants. I watched his face go from a healthy brown color to no color, and I knew he was dying.... We finally stopped. I gently put him down and cradled him in my arms. The chief came over. He was crying. So was the other uncle. We all cried as we watched that little, innocent boy die."

Tears squeezed from beneath his thick, spiky black lashes. Rafe felt the knot of grief surge up his throat. It was as if Ari sensed his need to cry, for her hand came to rest on the back of his head in a stroking gesture. That one touch triggered an avalanche of sorrow from him. He sobbed once, hard, against her shoulder.

"Let it go," Ari murmured. "I'll just hold you...let it go. Give your sadness to me, Rafe...."

A second sob was wrenched from deep within him; it felt as if someone were tearing his guts out by hand. He held her hard, as if to release her would be to drown in a hell he couldn't keep from overpowering him. Her arms tightened around him, comforting and nurturing. Oh, how long he had wished for a woman whose heart and soul were strong enough to hold him in his worst moments of need. He pressed his face against her neck, her hair silken and fragrant against his cheek.

Ari held him hard against her. He was nearly twice her size, but that didn't matter. As the choked, weeping sounds tore out of him, she understood finally what Inca had been telling her all week. She understood what power meant. Right now, she was able to connect with Rafe and knew she was much stronger than he at the moment. He needed her. With each sob, his hands gripped her shoulders with almost painful intensity. There was something cleansing and beautiful to Ari about the realization that she could be a safe haven in the storm of his life. He had nearly died. How close he'd come!

Pressing her head against his, whispering words of encouragement to him to help him divest himself of the monstrous event that he held so deep within him, Ari felt hot tears rolling down her cheeks and mingling with his. Life and death were so closely entwined down here in Amazonia. Ari had sensed the danger Rafe was in, and now it was confirmed. As she held him, rocked him, she couldn't envision her life without him being a part of it.

In the darkness, with the lightning sending pale shadows skittering across the hold of the houseboat, Ari realized that she *was* falling in love with Rafe. He had entrusted her with his vulnerability, shared his tears, his grief, with her. And she savored the gift as she rocked and soothed him. This she knew how to do. An incredible euphoria cascaded through her even as her heart was breaking over the boy's needless death. Life was so precious down here, yet so fragile.

Without thinking, Ari released her hold and slid her hands upward to frame his face. As he eased away, his lashes beaded with tears, his eyes dark with agony, she leaned upward and pressed her mouth against his. She felt him quiver savagely. She tasted the salt of his spent tears as her lips slid firmly against his. All she wanted to do was touch him in this most intimate of ways, take some of the horror away by sharing her strength, her love with him. Her small hands were firm upon his face and she accepted the pressure of his strong mouth as he hungrily kissed her in return. Her breathing snagged. Her heart soared as she felt his hands grip her shoulders. Suddenly he leaned back against the bulkhead, taking her with him until she lay across his torso, her mouth locked with his as if destined to do so.

Time ceased to exist. His mouth was conquering,

taking and giving back to her. Only vaguely aware of his hands moving from her upper arms and curving around the sides of her aching breasts, she boldly plundered his mouth in return. She wanted him to know how deeply he moved her, how much he meant to her. Words were useless. Showing him, not telling him, was the only way Ari could communicate with him. He smelled of lime-scented soap, the clean perspiration at his hairline, and tasted strongly male to her ripening, exploding senses.

As his hands brushed the curve of her breasts, Ari moaned and broke away from his mouth. His touch was exquisite. Fiery. Her nipples hardened instantly against his chest. Opening her eyes, she was captured and mesmerized by the way he gazed at her through obsidian, glittering, half-opened eyes. In that instant, she felt as if she were the prey and he the consummate and powerful predator. As a flash of lightning illuminated the cabin, she saw the primal desire of a man for his woman in the depths of his eyes.

Trembling beneath his caressing touch, Ari pushed away. "No...Rafe..." she protested, giving in to her own fear. Afraid she would disappoint Rafe, who was so worldly and obviously schooled in how to love a woman, Ari pulled back. She saw his brows dip and the burning light in his eye snuff out. His hands jerked away from her breasts as if he'd been scalded.

Ari sat there breathing hard, her hand against her mouth. "I—I'm sorry, Rafe.... I only meant to comfort you...." Tears dribbled from her eyes.

Groaning, Rafe whispered, "Come here, *mi flor.* It is I who owe you an apology. A gentleman does not presume. I am in the wrong, not you...." And he was. What had he been thinking? To love her was to commit completely to her. In his country, an honorable man did not take a woman to bed—until after marriage. No, he would not defile Ari in this way. He must release her. But he could not just yet, and Ari reluctantly allowed herself to be embraced by him. He felt the rigidity in her and closed his eyes as he held her for just one greedy moment more. He was such a damn thief. He'd never treated any woman as he was treating Ari. Rafe had been schooled to always ask a woman for her permission for a kiss, and to treat her with the utmost respect. Tonight, he'd presumed. Too much, he told himself harshly. Far too much.

The thunder caromed overhead, shaking the houseboat. More lightning arced and danced around them. Then the rain started—huge drops, then smaller staccato ones striking the deck above. Rafe released Ari. There was no place to go. Ordinarily, he'd have excused himself and left, but it was raining hard now. Easing her away from him, his hands lingering on her shoulders, he tried to smile at her, but didn't succeed.

"Thank you for being here for me," he told her quietly, his voice hoarse from the hard weeping. "I shouldn't have taken advantage of you. I should have realized what you were doing—comforting me."

"Rafe, no..."

"Hush, *mi flor.*" He gave her a sad smile. "In a month or two, you will be gone. I will be here again, alone. We should not start something that we cannot finish, no?" Sliding his fingers through the softness of her golden hair, he murmured gruffly, "I have no right to touch you as a man does his woman. I know better. Somehow…being with you makes me forget myself, my being a gentleman. I hope you can forgive me?"

Giving him a tender look, Ari felt bereft as he pulled his hands away from her. Her scalp tingled pleasantly where he'd sifted her hair through his long, strong fingers. His words haunted her. He was right: she'd be gone soon. And it wouldn't be fair to Rafe to start something intimate and then just walk away from him. The sadness on his face made her want to cry. As never before, Ari understood how alone he was. How many times had he seen children murdered? How many times had he brushed death himself? How many times had he lain here, alone, without someone to soothe him? Hold him? Love him when he felt so grief stricken and in need of another's touch to convince him that life was worth living, no matter what he'd seen or experienced?

Chewing on her lower lip, Ari moved off his bed and stood in the narrow aisle, her cotton gown wrinkled and plastered against her body. "You're right, Rafe. I see that now…."

"Try and sleep," he urged. "We're both tired and strung out."

Settling into her bed, Ari mutely agreed, though

her body throbbed and ached without remission. She wanted to love him. To feel the power of him deeply within herself. But she was going to be gone in a month or two. Lying down, she glumly pulled the sheet across her body and faced the bulkhead, her back toward Rafe. As she lay there wide awake, his words haunted her. What did she really want? Just the thought of leaving Rafe made her queasy. She loved this place. She loved the Amazon. Yet she had her mother's dream to fulfill. She couldn't do both. Real life, the responsibilities, the promises she'd made, became muddled within her. Closing her eyes, her hand pressed beneath her cheek, she sighed painfully.

Chapter Nine

Rafe tried to keep his face carefully arranged so that his unhappiness would not show. Today Ari was leaving for Manaus, to catch a flight back to New York City, to try and sell her book. Where had three months gone? He sat up on the deck, paperwork on his lap, the sun's rays muted by the wispy white clouds that hung low over the jungle at this time of morning. Only a few feet away were several scarlet ibis, their scimitar beaks busily searching the muddy shoals of the Amazon for food, their red plumage breathtaking against the brown backdrop of slow-moving water.

His heart ached. Ever since he'd held Ari in his arms that night, and sobbed out his grief over the loss of the boy and his father, Rafe and Ari had kept a comfortable distance from one another. He'd been out of line to recklessly and selfishly kiss her. Chastising himself for his one moment of weakness, Rafe had made damned sure that he wouldn't force himself upon Ari in that way again. Every time he wanted to reach out and touch her shoulder, or embrace her in a moment of discovery and joy, he stopped himself. But it was a sweet hell he lived in.

Looking down at the report he'd been reading, the paper wrinkled beneath his damp hand, he scowled. Rafe sternly told himself that he'd known from the beginning that Ari's stay would be short-lived. Why had he harbored the idea that she'd fall in love with him? With Amazonia? She was on a mission and he recognized that. Ari had to fulfill the dream of her dead mother before she could be free to pursue other things in life that beckoned to her. Still, his heart hurt with the knowledge that in a few hours, a tugboat from Manaus would be coming to pick Ari up and take her away—forever—from his encampment. From him.

Compressing his mouth against the pain, he dipped his head and scribbled notes on the papers spread across his knees. He could hear Ari moving around down below. This morning she would not be joining him for breakfast at the campfire. Every day up until now he would make eggs and fry bacon and she would make toast and coffee. It was a simple pleasure he'd come to look forward to like a child looked forward to opening gifts on Christmas morning.

When he heard Ari climbing the steps, he raised his head. She emerged, her blond hair drawn back into a thick, gold knot at the nape of her neck. Today she wore a cream tank top, a peach-colored linen blazer and trousers. She looked more formal, more of the North American world of privilege she'd come from than the home she'd made in Amazonia. Usually she wore a pair of khaki shorts that displayed her legs to wonderful advantage, a colorful tank top, her hair drawn up off her neck and shoulders in a playful ponytail. Every few days he'd find a small orchid and give it to her so that she could affix it to her hair.

"How's the packing coming?" he asked, keeping his tone light and teasing.

Ari wrinkled her nose as she eased herself up onto the splintery, unpainted surface of the deck. "Okay, I guess," she replied, standing next to Rafe and gazing at the scarlet ibis. "I'll miss seeing them every morning," she admitted, pushing several crinkly strands of hair behind her ear. The humidity was high this morning; Rafe had said that the rainy season was about to begin. Pursing her lips, Ari glanced at him. How handsome Rafe looked. She'd known him long enough now to realize the darkness she saw in his eyes was pain. How many times in the last three months had she seen that look? Rafe's job was fraught with danger, she had discovered. And the drug runners were relentless in kidnapping older children and women to be used as slaves in the cocaine factories hidden far to the north in steep, nearly impassable valleys wedged tightly between the green-clad mountains.

Flexing the fingers of her right hand, Ari stopped herself from reaching out to slide them across Rafe's shoulder. He wore a short-sleeved khaki shirt and trousers, as he did every day. The patches on each arm proclaimed his authority in the region.

"Three months have flown by," Rafe said, as he slowly gathered papers scattered on the deck and collected them into his lap.

The scarlet ibis were suddenly startled by something Ari couldn't see or hear. They took off in a flapping cloud of crimson and deep pink as the sunlight shone through their arcing wings. The display left her breathless, as it always did. There was such color, such life, here.

"I know," she murmured. "I'm going to miss it. All of it." And she turned and looked toward the campfire. The tug was to arrive at 8:00 a.m., in less than an hour. She saw the coffeepot perking on the edge of the coals. "Join me for one last cup of coffee?"

He smiled tenderly. "Of course." Rising, he took the report and slid it into a cardboard file nearby. Watching as Ari confidently moved down the plank to the riverbank, Rafe felt joy wind through him. She now walked with her shoulders squared, her chin up. That week with Inca had changed her from her mouselike self. Over the past weeks, he'd watched Ari bloom. She took risks. She was fearful sometimes, but she never let fear stop her as it had before.

Once he'd taken her to a mountain to the north, and they had spent three days climbing the rugged, jungle-clad slopes in search of orchids. Ari had a fear of heights, but that didn't stop her as it once had. Rafe had watched her handle the fear, move through it and emerge victorious. The orchids she drew in those three days were some of her best work. As he watched Ari's confidence and self-esteem grow, he was proud and happy for her. At the same time, Rafe battled his own personal fear of seeing her leave, because she would no longer need him.

Joining her at the campfire, he took the tin cup she proffered. Sitting down on a log, Rafe watched her greedily, wanting to imprint her every graceful movement, every expression, like a brand into his aching heart. He loved her. It was so simple, yet heartbreaking. Ari couldn't know that, either. Rafe would not presume to tell her. He knew she cared for him deeply. Still, she had to continue her odyssey. To confess something like that to her now would be wrong. And more than anything, Rafe wanted her to have a successful completion of her journey.

Ari settled next to Rafe, their elbows barely brushing. With her tin cup wrapped in both hands, she gazed fondly at the river. Two squadrons of brightly colored parrots swooped overhead. Then a white egret, a cousin to the great blue heron, came winging by, slow and graceful, on the lookout for frogs along the banks of the river.

"I'm going to miss all this," she admitted softly. "The quiet. The beauty. New York City is noisy, dirty and polluted. People are crushed together, unrelenting waves of humanity on the sidewalks, in the subways...."

Rafe gave her a sideways glance. "It is a different world, *mi flor.*"

She managed a painful half smile. Drowning in the warmth of his gaze, she uttered, "And more than anything, I'm going to miss you, Rafe." Ari felt the words jam up in her throat. Her heart felt heavy in her breast. "I—there's so much I want to say to you, Rafe, but the time—it isn't right and I know it. I have to go home. I have to try and sell the book... and face my father...."

"Shh, *mi flor,*" he whispered, his voice catching. "I understand. More than you realize."

After searching his sad features, Ari's gaze dropped to his strong, wonderful mouth. The corners were drawn inward with pain. That was how she felt, too. "I'm going to miss how you share your feelings with me. It has been so easy living here with you. And I feel like I've grown a decade by being here. I feel different, in a good way, about myself now." She tore her gaze from his, sipped her coffee and stared out at the river. "When I came, I was a shy little shadow running away from myself. I didn't believe in me. I didn't believe I could draw one orchid, much less forty of them. Leaving here today, I feel strong and good, Rafe. About myself. About the book that you've helped me with so much." She smiled at him. "The stories you've given me as text really make the drawings of the orchids come alive.

They aren't just pretty pictures. There is meaning, legend and symbology behind each one of them."

He nodded. "Chief Aroka helped us a lot, too, don't forget."

"Don't worry, when I sell this book, my acknowledgement page is going to have the names of everyone who helped me. Especially Inca, who gave me the incredible gift of just being herself. What a role model she's been to me." Ari's gaze softened. "And you'll be the first person I name." Unable to help herself, she reached over and slid her hand over his, where it rested on his knee. She saw him tense momentarily. They'd not touched one another since that fateful night when he'd wept in her arms. Oh, how she longed to have him touch her again! But Ari was mature enough to know that she didn't want to lead Rafe on like that. It wasn't fair to him—or to her.

Gripping her fingers in his, Rafe gave her a gentle smile in return. "Getting the book sold should be your only focus now."

Reluctantly, Ari withdrew her fingers. "I bought a writer's reference book that has all the publishers listed. I made an A list of ten of them that I'm going to contact as soon as I land in New York. I don't know what will happen, or even if the editors will see me or not. But I've got to try...." A heated sensation throbbed in her lower body. How many times had she wondered what it would be like to love Rafe? And then the fear that she would never be good enough, that she would fail, inevitably chilled her.

Slipping his hand back around the tin cup he held, Rafe said confidently, "All you have to do is show them your exquisite drawings, and they will be helpless to say anything but yes to publishing your book."

Ari laughed. "That's not how real-life publishing goes, from my understanding. No, I'm prepared to knock on a lot of doors and get a lot of no's flung in my face. It might take weeks...even months to get it sold, but that's what I'll do."

"And your father? How do you think he's going to react to you being in New York by yourself? You said he expects you to come home to your apartment in Georgetown?"

"Mmm, that." Ari sighed and frowned. "He's my biggest obstacle, Rafe. Every time I think of him, of having to call him once I land in the U.S., my stomach clenches. I thought about using the Iridium phone, but I just needed this time alone. I did write him several letters, though. I'm afraid. I'm afraid I'll kowtow to him just like before." With a shake of her head, she murmured, "Inca made me realize in her own way that my father has me—or had me—under his thumb. I was his do-bee. Do this. Do that. Do his bidding. Do what he wanted. Well—" she pushed several strands away from her eyes "—I can't go home and do that. I have to be strong enough to stand up to him."

"Yes," Rafe said quietly, "there comes a time in everyone's life where they must leap out of the nest and fly on their own."

She nodded. "You did that with your father when you walked away from his plans for you, from the business he wanted you to eventually run."

"There's a price to pay," Rafe said carefully. "I only hope your father will not be as pigheaded as mine was, and disown you because you want to have a life of your own after your book sells. I hope he doesn't expect you to work on Wall Street and crunch numbers." He smiled at her. She looked exquisite this morning, her lips soft and slightly parted, her eyes the color of the pale sky above them, with gold in their depths. Rafe knew how happy Ari was here. The rain forest had embraced her, had loved her, and she had loved it in return. And now she was leaving.

Ari was about to speak when she heard the *chut-chut-chut* of a tug coming. Standing up, cup in hand, she craned her neck. Sure enough, a brightly painted red-and-white tug was chugging up the channel toward the houseboat. For a moment, she felt a keen thrill of excitement, like that of a knife slicing through her heart. And simultaneously, she felt like crying. She didn't want to leave Rafe. Ari was fairly sure that she loved him. Oh, they'd never spoken about it. No, since that catalytic night in the hold, he'd backed off, given her room and kept their friendship warm but without the touches and kisses of before.

How much she missed all that! Setting the cup down on the log, she gave Rafe a helpless smile. "My taxi is here...."

Rising, he said, "Let me get your luggage for you. I'll transfer it to the tug."

Standing there, she watched Rafe move toward their home. And it was a home for Ari. Fighting back tears, she gulped unsteadily. Forcing herself to move, she slowly followed him.

Rafe moved the luggage to the tug. The captain, a dark-skinned Indian by the name of Pablo, his front teeth missing, helped Rafe put the luggage on the deck. Ari stood on shore, her heart beating hard in her chest. Beneath her arm, encased in plastic, were the four sketchbooks filled with orchids she'd drawn for the book.

"Just a moment," Rafe told her, and he trotted quickly back to the houseboat and up the ramp.

Puzzled, Ari watched as he moved to the cockpit. As he emerged, he was smiling and holding something in his large hand. As he strode down the ramp and over to where she stood, her eyes widened enormously. There, in his hand, was an incredible orchid she'd never seen before.

"Oh, Rafe!" she cried, reaching out as he handed it gently to her.

Seeing the joy in her eyes, the way her mouth lifted, he felt his heart exploding in his chest. There was everything to love about Ari, from her innocent reactions to the beauty of the orchids to her powerful response to life—and to him. As their fingers met and touched, he placed the blossom, actually a spray of four, each one white with a pink lip, into her hand.

"Here, *mi flor,* a parting gift from my heart to

your heart,'' he whispered, as he held her luminous gaze. ''This is *Encyclia randii*. I purposely did not show this one to you because I knew you would leave, and the legend about it belongs to someone who goes away. When a man gives a woman this orchid, he hopes that she will one day return to him.'' His fingers closed carefully over hers and over the orchid. As he held her tearful gaze, his voice broke. ''The man, as the legend goes, hopes that by giving the woman he cares for the orchid, she will one day, at the right time, present it back to him upon her return. This is the orchid of farewell and new beginnings. I want you to have it…. It's very rare….''

Choking on a sob, Ari stared at the orchid. ''Look at the colors, Rafe. It's so incredibly beautiful….''

''Hauntingly beautiful. More ghost than real,'' he agreed in a quiet tone. She was so close. He wanted to kiss her goodbye. His head said no, to keep his distance. Yet as Rafe looked up into her eyes and saw the tears fall across her flushed cheeks, he moved forward.

Taking Ari into his arms, mindful she had the sketchpads beneath her left arm and the orchid in her right hand, he slid his hands along her shoulders. ''May I kiss you goodbye?'' he asked huskily.

Ari quivered as his strong, capable fingers slid along her linen-jacketed shoulders. ''Yes…oh, yes… please?'' she whispered, and leaned up on tiptoe, her breasts brushing against his chest.

Groaning softly, Rafe slid his hand upward along

her long, slender neck and framed her face. Looking deeply into her tear-damp eyes, he leaned down... down to capture her orchidlike lips, which were parted, bathed in her tears and waiting for him.

His world centered only on Ari. On her mouth opening like the ripe blossom of an orchid to the rays of sunlight as he connected with her. Sliding his mouth tenderly along hers, like a butterfly brushing them, he whispered, "You are in my heart, Ari. You always will be...."

As his mouth took hers more strongly, she moaned and sank against his tall, strong body. She could taste the coffee on his mouth, the scent of the lime soap he'd used in his recent shower. Her heart soared. More tears fell, met and melded against their clinging mouths. Never had she loved anyone as she loved Rafe. And she had to leave him.

Rafe eased his mouth from hers. He tasted the salt of her tears upon his lips. Gently smoothing the tendrils of hair around her face, he tried to smile and failed. "Once the orchid begins to die, press it for me? And when you want, bring it back to me. I'll be here, waiting for it...and you...."

Ari cried off and on throughout the flight back to the United States. When Condor Airlines landed at JFK International Airport, she walked as if she had a million pounds of fear upon her shoulders. When she realized she was becoming like her old self again, her shoulders rounded, her head hanging down, she gave herself a good talking to. After Rafe had given her the orchid, she'd attached the spray to her hair, and every so often she would touch it to ensure that it was still in place. Touching it was almost like having Rafe beside her.

After she made her way through Customs, and then out into the airy terminal packed with thousands of human beings like bees coming and going from their hive, Ari retrieved her luggage. Weighted down, she glumly walked outside. Night had fallen and in the distance she could see the brightly lit skyline of Manhattan. This was her destiny. Grimly she flung back her shoulders and forced herself to lift her chin. If Inca saw her so down, she'd pounce on her like a jaguar and give her a chastising she'd not soon forget.

Making her step more confident, Ari sought out a cabbie and got into his bright yellow vehicle. Her plans for New York had been made before she'd left for Brazil. She'd done her homework on which hotel she wanted to stay in. The Sunflower Hotel was located in the heart of New York, near where most publishers had offices.

Tiredness ate at her. The flight had been long and exhausting. She wished to be home, with Rafe, at the houseboat. Already she missed him so much. Ari had relied on his levelheaded maturity. He'd been a wonderful and patient teacher. And how she'd grown beneath his nurturing!

Rubbing her chest, her heart aching without respite, Ari forced herself to think ahead. Once she got to the hotel at 42nd Street and Lexington, she would have to call her father and let him know she was back. Her stomach clenched. What would he say?

"Ari! You're back. Thank God."

Ari stood over the phone next to her bed in the hotel. Her heart was beating with fear. "Hi, Father. How are you?"

"I'm fine. But you? Where are you calling from? Are you at your Georgetown condo?"

Her heart fell. Her fingers wrapped spasmodically around the phone. "No...I'm not. I'm in New York City. Remember? I told you that after I got the drawings completed, and the text, I was going to try and sell the book?"

"You're where?"

She closed her eyes and sat down on the edge of the queen-size bed. He hadn't changed one whit in three months. And Ari felt like she was a new person, in comparison to him. "Father, nothing has changed. I'm staying in New York until I can sell my book."

"Don't tell me you managed to actually draw orchids?" She heard the sarcasm in his deep voice.

At first Ari was crushed. And then anger flared inside her. She remembered what Inca had said about people who wanted to disempower her; that it was up to her to first recognize it, then stop it, and keep her own truth at the center of her heart. Moving the phone from her right hand to her left, she allowed the anger to be heard in her voice. The old Ari would have cowed and spoke in a soft, apologetic tone. She didn't do that now.

"Father, it's obvious you don't think I'm capable of doing anything on my own. I may not have my mother's talent, but I can draw orchids pretty well. Anyway, an editor will determine that, not you or me."

"Don't you get snotty with me, young lady—"

"I'm not being snotty. I'm being honest. You're not taking away from me what I've done," she said, her voice wobbling with anger.

"What the hell has gotten into you, Ari? Who do you think you're talking to? I'm footing all your damn bills for this little escapade. The least you owe me is respect, not anger."

Shaking now, the adrenaline flooding through her, Ari sat with her right fist clenched on her lap. "That's another thing I was going to talk to you about, Father. I'm staying here in New York and I'll get a job. I don't care if it's a menial job or not. I'm staying in this city, making the rounds, knocking on doors until I get this book sold."

"Dammit, Ari! Has going down to Brazil made you crazy?"

Tears jammed her eyes. She scrunched them shut and forced the tears back. This was not a time to cry. Her father always took her tears as a sign of weakness. But right now, she felt scared and over-whelmed. Recalling how many times Rafe had placed himself in real danger for others fueled her. Ari had a mission to accomplish for her mother. She saw her father as an enemy trying to stop her. "Yes, it's made me crazy! I've finally gotten out from beneath your thumb, Father. I've had three months to find out who Ari Worthington is. And I'm not going to cower any more. I'm going ahead with this dream of mine."

"You've lost your senses, young lady! Now, I'm going to send one of my attachés up there and—"

Ari slammed the phone down. She sat there, shaking visibly. Fists tight in her lap, she tried to breathe deeply, to center herself as Inca had taught her. Within a minute, she felt calmer. Her heart was settling back down. Reaching over, she touched the waxy, thick petals of the orchid Rafe had given her, which now sat in a small glass of water on the bedstand. She could almost feel his smile, his approval of her standing up to her father.

"Well, I've burned all my bridges, Rafe and Inca. You're probably cheering me on, and I'm scared to death...." Looking around, worried and fretting, Ari knew that her hundred-dollar-a-night hotel room would have to go, and soon. She'd saved some money, but not enough to stay in such a place for long. No, she'd have to get a job—fast. Looking around the Victorian-style room, she chewed on her lower lip. How she wished Rafe was here. He made her feel strong, as if she could accomplish anything she set out to do.

Lonely as never before, Ari got up and started to unpack her sketchbooks. She brought them back to the bed and sat down, the first one across her lap.

One day, when Rafe was working on his reports at the campfire, she'd made a sketch of him. She'd never shown it to him for fear he'd laugh at her. Turning to that page, she sighed as she studied the sketch. He was in profile, his face clean and strong looking. She had many canisters of film yet to be developed, including a number of photographs of him, but Ari knew she'd have to get a job first in order to be able to afford the processing.

Briefly touching his tousled black hair, she closed her eyes and imagined that she was threading her fingers through his hair once more, as she had that night she'd held him. That night was indelibly branded upon her heart, her spirit. No man had ever trusted her enough to cry in her arms. Rafe was so different from all the other men she'd encountered in her life thus far. Opening her eyes, she glumly looked around the room.

Well, tomorrow a new chapter in her life would begin; she had to find a job and then start knocking on editors' doors. Frightened as never before, Ari knew she'd have to walk through her fear and keep her eyes on her dream. Glancing at the orchids, she wanted more than anything to be home with Rafe. In Amazonia. Was that a dream, too? Could she make it come true? Rafe wanted her back. He had not said he loved her, but in her heart, she knew he did. And she thought she understood why he hadn't said those words to her. He was a throwback to ages past, when a man was a courtly gentleman. A Victorian era aristocrat who respected her completely.

Enough to allow her the freedom to follow her dream of having her book published.

As Ari listlessly stood and opened her suitcase to find her nightgown, she remembered Rafe telling her that if love was real between a man and a woman, it allowed each of them to walk their own path. That marriage, to him, was a partnership, and that each partner had to respect the other's passions and dreams. Well, he was giving her that freedom now. And he'd given her an orchid that was an open invitation to go back home. How desperately she wanted to! Being in a large city, alone, without friends or help, was daunting. Yet Ari knew she had to do this. Inca had told her that there were tests in everyone's life, where they had to walk a gauntlet of fire alone. Those that had the heart, the faith in themselves and the driving need to reach their goals would survive.

A new sense of determination flowed through Ari. It was surprising, and yet she welcomed it. Over the next few minutes, she felt a trickle of hope that she would be able to meet her adversity face-to-face. As Inca had said, all she had to do was *try*. That was all that was asked of anyone. Even if she failed, that didn't mean she'd lost anything. But if she didn't try, she would be a failure. Buoyed by Inca's words, and Rafe's unspoken love for her, Ari took in a deep breath. On the bedstand was the orchid. All she had to do was look at it, hear Rafe's emotion-filled request that she come back to him, and that was enough....

Chapter Ten

"Father?"

Ben Worthington was working at his massive cherry desk in the Pentagon late on a snowy December afternoon. It was Friday, and most people had left early because of the snowstorm that was stalking the East Coast. He hadn't; there was too much paperwork to catch up on. When he heard his daughter's strong, clear voice, his head snapped up. Ari stood in the open doorway, his assistant, Becky, standing behind her, an apologetic look on her face. No one saw the secretary of the Navy without an appointment, even his daughter, who had disappeared out of his life in July.

Clearing his throat, he nodded to his assistant. "That's all right, Becky. Bring us some cookies and coffee, please?'' He stood, feeling anger and curiosity and relief mix violently within himself as Ari moved into the office. She was wearing a soft pink wool beret, her golden hair tucked beneath the camel hair coat that fell to her knees. She wore black wool slacks and a pair of black galoshes still shiny with melting snow. The vivid purple wool muffler thrown around her neck and shoulders made her blue eyes seem even larger.

''Ari...'' he murmured, coming around the desk, his hands outstretched. ''I've been worried sick about you.'' He stopped about six feet away from her. What was different about his daughter? Many things, he realized, beginning with the look in her eyes. He no longer saw fright there, and she was able to meet and hold his gaze. The way she held herself was different, too. Instead of being slump-shouldered, as if ashamed of something, she stood confidently before him, her chin uplifted. She gripped a large parcel wrapped in plastic against her breast.

''I'm fine, Father,'' she answered unsteadily. It took all of Ari's courage to meet his hard, assaulting gaze. That look of the eagle in her father's eyes had always scared her, but now she had to move through that fear. She saw him hesitate, his brows knitted in confusion. And then he dropped his hand and looked suddenly very old, his skin gray, not its normal ruddy color. Still, he looked strong and powerful in his expensive Italian pinstripe suit and ebony leather shoes. The tie was a paisley blue, black and cream design, equally conservative.

"This is quite a surprise," he uttered, and then saw his assistant rushing in with a silver tray filled with coffee cups and cookies. Smiling faintly, he gestured to the leather wing chair nearest him. "Have a seat, Ari. Becky will serve us and then we'll talk."

Ari swallowed hard. She was afraid of her father. After hanging up on him so many months ago and not contacting him since, she figured he would be furious with her. Now he appeared worried, yet grateful that she'd showed up. Gripping the parcel, she walked toward the chair only after he'd backed away, walked around the desk and sat down. Her hands moved nervously over the package as she placed it on the wing chair and divested herself of her coat, beret and muffler.

Becky smiled, took her wraps and then quietly closed the door and left them alone. Ari started to sit down.

"Would you like some coffee? Maybe cookies? Becky keeps my favorite around here even though I don't need them." Ben pointed to the chocolate-covered macaroons sitting in the center of the tray.

Ari gulped, feeling edgy. She had expected her father to start yelling at her, demanding to know why she'd walked out of his life. As she moved hesitantly toward the tray that sat on the coffee table on one side of the huge room, Ari realized that her father had aged more than a little. There was a lot more silver at the temples of his military short dark hair, and the silver in the natural wave dipping rebelliously down his perpetually wrinkled brow was more pronounced as well.

Ben watched his daughter covertly, pretending to look at several reports that needed his perusal and signature. "Your hair is a lot longer than I remember," he said pleasantly.

Ari politely took a cup of coffee and moved to the wing chair. "I know. Being that it's cold now, I'm glad it's long. It keeps me warmer," she said with a soft laugh. After placing the cup and saucer on the edge of his desk, she picked up her parcel once again and sat down. Her heart pounded, underscoring her fear. At any moment, she knew, he could fly into a rage at her. She saw the confusion, the hurt and anger in his narrowed blue eyes. Compressing her lips, she inhaled deeply and said, "I came here for a reason, Father."

"Yes, I can see that," he said. Placing his pen into the inkwell, he folded his hands in front of him. "What's in the package you're holding on to like your life depends upon it?"

Her lips lifted in a little smile. He was teasing her. For just a moment, all his armor dissolved and he lost the tough expression from his bulldog features. "It's the galley proofs on my orchid book, which I wrote for Mom."

Stunned, Ben stared at her, and then at the parcel wrapped in clear plastic to protect it from the winter weather. "Book?"

Ari stood and walked to his desk. With careful authority, she placed the package on the cherry wood and opened it, one corner at a time. "Yes. I wanted to share the good news with you. You know how Mom loved to paint orchids. I know I can never be the artist she was, but a publisher finally bought it." Smoothing the plastic away from the enclosed page proofs, a three-inch-thick bundle, she slowly turned it around so that he could take a look if he wanted to. Ari hoped and prayed that he would.

"I'll be damned," he muttered, reaching for the top galley and pulling it toward him.

Ari bit her lower lip and forced herself to sit down. Out of nervousness, she picked up the coffee and took several scalding sips. After he'd slowly leafed through the first few pages, his hand froze. Her heart plummeted.

Ben read aloud the dedication in the book: "To my mother, Ellen Hanover-Worthington, orchid artist. This book is dedicated to her, and to all the new species of orchids that were found in Brazil, in the Amazon Basin. May her name and her love of them live on forever."

Lifting his chin, he narrowed his eyes on Ari. "A very nice dedication. I know your mother would have liked it." His words were filled with emotion.

A frisson of terror came and went. Ari gripped the coffee cup that she held rigidly above her lap. "Go on. Look at the first chapter...." Now she really felt fear, because he would look upon her orchid drawings for the first time. The publisher had made color copies of them for the galley; the real photos taken from the originals were at the printer's, ready to be processed for printing.

Ben leafed through several more pages. When he came upon Ari's first colored drawing, his mouth dropped open. His hands hovered in midair, the sketch in his fingers. Brows rising in surprise, he stared at it. And then he looked over at his daughter. "This…is *your* work, Ari?" Ben saw so much of Ellen's style in Ari's work. And yet there was Ari's own unique expression in the strokes, in the way she connected colors and shades into a drawing that looked more real than real life. He was stunned.

"All mine," she laughed nervously. "There's thirty sketches in there. All done with the same colored pencil set Mom gave me that last year before she died." She wanted to ask "What do you think?" but was too cowardly to do so. Her father's expression was one of frank shock. Did he like them? Hate them? Ari was unsure, and she wished that she didn't care as much as she did whether or not he would approve of them.

Silence settled around them like a thick, warm blanket on that cold, snowy afternoon. Ben took his time leafing through the pages of the book. On some, he studied Ari's pencil sketches and saw that they were simple, straightforward and yet graceful and shouting of her love of the subjects she drew. As well as the beautiful orchids, there might be a vine twisting down the trunk of a tree, or a white egret standing in the shallows of a channel, looking for frogs. And then he began to read some of the notes opposite her sketches.

"How long did this take you?" he murmured as he continued to page through the manuscript.

"Three months. Rafe helped me a lot. And so did the Juma Indians, who would take me out and show me all those beautiful orchids."

"These are—" he looked up, his voice tinged with awe "—incredible, Ari. Simply incredible." With a sweep of his hand, he added, "You're better than your mother. Do you realize that?"

Her heart thudded. "Oh, no, Father. I'll never have anywhere near mother's skill and talent!" Yet joy flooded through her. He liked her drawings! It was more than Ari dared hope for. Ben Worthington could have started screaming and yelling at her like he usually did, but this time was different. Maybe because she was different, she mused. During the last five months she had matured in many, many ways. The confidence that had taken root in Amazonia had been nurtured, tempered, challenged and solidified by working in New York City at the library at New York University.

Ben placed his hands over the manuscript and looked at his daughter. "I owe you an apology, Ari. I said you weren't an artist, but you are. You might not have gone to college to learn your craft, but you learned it from your mother." His voice softened and he shook his head. "How much you've become like her."

Sitting very quietly, holding her coffee cup, Ari

couldn't believe her ears. Her father had always put her down. Now he was complimenting her. What had changed? Looking up, she said, "What is so different between when I phoned you in July and now? The fact that you've seen my work?"

Ben leaned back in his chair. It creaked in protest. With one hand lying across her galley proofs, he looked up at the ceiling for a moment. His voice was filled with apology and regret when he finally spoke. "Ari, when your mother died, you were very young. I didn't have a clue how to raise you. Kirk, yes, because he was a boy...male. But Ellen had always raised you girls. When she died, well, I...felt useless. Helpless as a matter of fact. I knew I couldn't mother you like she had. I was angry. Very angry that she was taken away from me...from all of us...at such a young age. I was heartbroken. I could barely function at my job as a naval officer, much less think two coherent thoughts about how to raise you and Kirk."

Sighing, he looked across the desk to Ari. "You more or less raised yourself, honey. You took over for your mother in many ways. I was gone so much on duty, and you kept the house clean, made meals for Kirk and me when I was home." Opening his hand, he whispered painfully, "When you hung up on me in July, I was furious with you. I was ready to call out the FBI, put out a tail to find you and drag you back here to Washington."

Ari gave him a surprised look.

He laughed self-consciously. "What I did instead

was call Morgan Trayhern. He's my age and has four
kids he's raising. I told him what had gone down
and I asked him for advice. What should I do with
a rebellious daughter who was fully intent on jumping out of the nest I'd made for her?'' He chuckled
ruefully and held her teary gaze.

''Morgan counseled me to leave you alone. He'd
warned me prior to you going to Brazil that you were
at an age where you needed to explore, to find out
who *you* were. He told me in no uncertain terms to
keep my mouth shut and let you leap out of the
nest.''

''I—see…''

''It's one of the hardest things I've ever done, Ari.
When you first left for the Amazon, I wanted to be
there to protect you. You're so young.''

She shrugged delicately. ''You can't keep protecting me for the rest of my life, Father. If you
hadn't let me go there, I wouldn't have done this.''
She pointed to the book. ''Come spring, it will be
published. I'm so excited.''

Smiling proudly at her, Ben covered the galley
proofs with his large hands. ''Was it hard finding a
publisher?''

''Very,'' she muttered, and sipped the coffee. ''I
got a job at an accounting firm. I'd make appointments to see editors at different houses on my lunch
break. I was turned down fifteen times in a row.''

Shaking his head, he marveled, ''Fifteen? You're
a lot stronger than I've given you credit for, Ari. You

kept at it, though, and you sold it." He brightened. "Are you getting millions for it?"

Laughing fully, Ari set the cup and saucer on the desk in front of her. "Millions? What a crock. Most writers would starve to death if they wrote one book a year. And ninety-nine percent of us get petty advances." She gestured to the book. "I got a five-thousand-dollar advance."

"Not exactly career building, is it? You couldn't walk away from your day job on that, could you?"

"Most writers never will," Ari said glumly. Then she brightened. "The editor says if the book sells well, they'll want a second one from me. The president of the American Society of Orchid Growers is going to give me an endorsement for the book cover. I've already been contacted by a very rich corporate owner who wants to bankroll me and send me back down to the Amazon to find new species of orchids for him and his collection in Florida. He said he's willing to pay me well to do this. I can find new orchids as I draw them for the next book, so it's a nice dovetailing. I'll get paid to do what I love best."

Frowning, Ben sat up. "But, Ari, what about your degree in business? I know I can get you a high-paying job on Wall Street—"

Holding up her hand, Ari said, "Father, please... I *love* what I did down in Amazonia."

"And?"

"And I wanted to come here this afternoon to tell you that I'm leaving tomorrow for Manaus. I'm going back down there, Father." She instantly saw anger darken his eyes. Steeling herself, she pushed on. "You need to know that I think I'm in love with Rafe Antonio. The man at whose camp I stayed." She opened her hands, excitement in her tone. "He's the most wonderful man I've ever met, not at all like the guys I've known here and in New York. He's been through so much and he's so levelheaded. He understands me, my dreams...."

Frowning, Worthington got out of his chair. He jammed his hands into his pants pockets and prowled the boundaries of his office for several seconds in silence. "Are you going back because you're pregnant?"

Gasping, Ari stared at her father. His face was hard. She was familiar with that look and it made her stomach clench in fear. "What?"

"You heard me," he growled.

The accusation stung her. Clenching her fists on her lap, Ari met his angry gaze. "What do you think I am? Someone who sleeps around with every man I see?"

"I didn't say that."

"Yes, you did!" Her voice rose in righteous indignation. "Rafe Antonio *never* made a play for me like you think, Father. He's a man of honor, with absolutely impeccable integrity. If you met him, you'd certainly change your mind about him. He's like a knight from the past. He would no more think of doing something like that to me than—than...oh, you make me really angry!" Ari jumped to her feet.

Surprised at herself, she froze. The glare her father

gave her caused her incredible agony. "You can see I'm not pregnant," she cried. "Rafe doesn't deserve that slap in the face and I sure don't, either!"

Wrestling with his anger, Ben snarled, "Then why the hell are you going back down there? Because this rich corporate tycoon is bankrolling you?"

Planting her hands on her hips, she faced her father squarely. "I'm going back down there to see what Rafe and I have together. Three months wasn't enough. I was under a lot of pressure then. Now that the book has been bought and is going to be published, I can start looking at my own dreams, Father. I feel like I've fulfilled my dream for Mom. For the family."

Raking his fingers through his hair, Ben stalked back to his desk. He jerked out the chair, sat down and looked at Ari. "I'm not giving you any money to do this. Not a penny."

Ari had expected that. Up until July, her father had always given her a generous amount of money every month. "You won't have to. I was coming in here to tell you that from now on, I'm on my own. You don't have to keep giving me money. I appreciate all you've done for me, Father, but it's time I made my own way."

"How are you going to pay for the flight down there, then?" he demanded.

"I've been saving money from my job," she told him defiantly. Her heart was beating with fear. Would he disown her, like Rafe's father had him, for going after what she wanted?

The harsh buzzing of the phone on his desk startled Ari. She saw her father's scowl deepen. Leaning over, he pressed the button.

"Yes, Becky?"

"I'm sorry to disturb you, Mr. Secretary, but Mr. Morgan Trayhern is here. He says it's urgent he see you."

Puzzled, Ben growled, "Send him in."

Ari moved to one side as the door swung open. She had heard of this very famous man through Rafe, who knew him personally. She watched as a tall, muscular man wearing a navy blue suit, white silk shirt and light blue tie stepped into the room. Morgan Trayhern radiated power.

Ben made introductions, then said, "This is unexpected, Morgan."

Morgan stood tensely, his hands clasped in front of him. "I know, Ben. I'm sorry to burst in on you without warning."

Scowling, Ben looked over at his daughter. "Ari, if you'll excuse us?"

"Wait," Morgan cautioned. "This concerns Ari. That's why I'm here."

Worthington said, "I don't understand."

"Neither do I," Ari murmured. She saw the agitation in Morgan's eyes, in the set of his mouth. Her stomach knotted.

"I knew you would be coming here today, Ms. Worthington," Morgan said in a low tone. "I was on my way here, to the Pentagon, on other business when I received an urgent satcom message on board our jet just before we landed at National Airport. My sources informed me you were coming in to see your father. That's why I knew where to reach you.''

''A call?'' Ari said. ''From who?''

Morgan clenched his fists and said, ''From Rafe. What you didn't know is that he had been assigned to protect you while you were down in Manaus. A bodyguard of sorts. Rafe wasn't going to do it until I told him your life could be in danger. It was then that he took the assignment.''

''You knew this?'' Ari looked at her father, stunned, and then at Morgan.

Worthington cleared his throat. ''I asked Morgan to provide you with someone who could not only help you in fulfilling your dream, Ari, but who could protect you. Rafe Antonio works undercover with Perseus, an organization Morgan owns.''

She stared at them. The silence was oppressive until she found her voice. ''Rafe…was…working for you? To guard me?'' Why hadn't he told her that? Her mind spun. Her heart tumbled.

''Rafe ordinarily would never have taken the assignment,'' Morgan told her gently. ''The only reason why he did is that I impressed upon him the possibility that your life could be in danger if you went into the Amazon looking for orchids with drug dealers around. He agreed on that premise alone, to protect you.''

''I—see…'' Helplessly, Ari opened her hands, she said, ''Well…why are you here, then? Is it about Rafe?''

"Yes," Morgan said heavily, "the satcom call I received was from Rafe, reporting that his camp was under heavy attack by the Valentino Brothers, local drug lords in that region." Apologetically, Morgan reached out and took her hand. "I hate breaking in here and telling you this, but I know Rafe means something to you. I just received a call from the police department in Manaus. They helicoptered down to his camp and found him wounded and unconscious."

Gasping, Ari jerked her hand away. "What? How is he? What else do you know?" She fought back a scream of denial as terror sizzled through her.

Morgan looked grave. "I don't know yet. I came over here as soon as I found out. The last transmission we received reported that Rafe was being flown back to Manaus, and a surgical team was on standby."

Ben studied Morgan in the shattering silence. "Wait a minute. How could you know where Ari was? If I didn't know, how would you?"

"Rafe, as part of his after-action report on the mission to protect Ari, told us she was going to New York City. She wrote him several letters since then, and we had her address." Morgan looked over at her. "We—I—had been keeping tabs on Ari's whereabouts because Rafe wanted to know how she was doing. He was worried about her being alone in New York, without money or support."

Ben cursed softly. "Dammit, Morgan, why didn't you tell me where she was? I've been sitting for five months, eating my guts out, wondering how I could locate her. My own daughter, dammit!''

Morgan said, ''Ben, I'm sorry. I didn't know you were out of touch or I'd have certainly told you where she was.''

Ari pressed her hand to her mouth. ''I've got to get on the first plane to Manaus. Mr. Trayhern… thank you for helping…'' She reached over, and grabbed the galley proofs. Inside she was shaking. Ari wanted to shriek to the heavens that this was all a bad joke, that Rafe couldn't be injured. But she knew only too well the danger he lived in down there and she knew the Valentino Brothers had a price on his head.

''Wait,'' Morgan pleaded. ''I'm getting the jet refueled right now. You can fly down with us, Ms. Worthington, if you want. Whenever one of my people gets wounded, I try to be there for them. Would you like to fly down with me?''

''Yes…yes, I would.'' Ari looked at her father. ''I have to go, Father. Rafe means a lot to me…I told you that.'' She saw the anguish in her father's eyes. He opened his mouth to protest, raised his hand and then dropped it, as if defeated.

''Yes,'' her father rasped, ''go with Morgan.''

Morgan reached over, his hand extended. ''I'm sorry to rain on your parade, Ben. I wish I was coming here with better news for both of you.''

Ben shook his hand and released it. He gazed forlornly in Ari's direction. ''Will you be coming home?''

Choking back a sob, Ari whispered, "I'm sure I will. I just don't know when. I care for Rafe, Father. Deeply. He's hurt. He might be dying. All I want to do right now is get down there and be at his side. He took care of me in so many ways when I needed someone to lean on. And now, I want to be there for him."

Morgan looked at his watch. "If we take off in the next hour, refuel in Mexico City, we should be down there in about six hours."

Relief skittered through her. "Good," Ari whispered brokenly. "Can we go, Mr. Trayhern?" She wanted to tear out of the office and run down the highly polished corridor. Rafe was wounded. How badly? Now Ari was filled with remorse. She'd never told Rafe she loved him. She'd never spoken of what lay in her heart because she'd been afraid. Was it too late?

Chapter Eleven

Ari tried to stifle a cry as she was admitted to the ICU of La Paloma Hospital in Manaus. Rafe lay amid instruments that beeped and sighed on either side of his bed, which was slightly raised. Her gaze flew to his face. She saw dark bruises and lacerations marring his handsome features. He was in a coma. His skin, once a vibrant color, was leached and pale. IVs were taped to both arms, the transparent plastic tubing dangling like limp spaghetti around him. Her hands went icy cold as the nurse closed the door behind her. The room was small and glass enclosed so that the nurses manning the station nearby could keep a watchful eye on all their patients who hovered in the wings of death. Gulping back tears, Ari walked unsteadily to Rafe's bedside. Her trembling fingers closed over his hand, which lay limply at his side, and she felt the coolness of his flesh. "Oh, no..." she moaned. Gripping his fingers, Ari leaned over and gently slid her other hand across his dark, mussed hair. How alive Rafe had been. Now it was as if his body was here, but his spirit was gone. Leaning over, Ari gently pressed her lips to his forehead and kissed him tenderly. His flesh was cool and damp. The doctors had told her and Morgan that Rafe had been shot in the back, and his liver was in shreds. Why he hadn't died on the helicopter ride back to Manaus, no one knew. The amount of blood he'd lost was significant. They did not hold much hope of Rafe coming out of the coma and surviving. According to the doctors, it was only a matter of time until he quietly slipped away into the waiting arms of death.

Tears leaked out of her tightly closed eyes as Ari rested her brow against his. Reeling with exhaustion, with fear, Ari whispered, "Rafe? It's me, Ari. I'm here, darling. I'm here for you. I'm so sorry you're so hurt, but I *know* you can beat this. Please... please...I love you." She halted, tears falling from her eyes. Tightening her grip on his listless fingers, she sobbed, "I love you. Do you hear me? I was afraid to say it when I was here before. I wasn't sure what love was at that time, Rafe. But I do now. Leaving you was the hardest thing I've ever done. My time in New York taught me what I didn't know." She pressed kiss after kiss across his unmarred brow. "Darling, I love you. I'd do *anything* to have you come back to me...."

Ari straightened up, wiped her eyes with the back of her hand and continued to touch Rafe's dark hair. He was a mere shadow of the vital man that he'd been before. Her knight... Was life going to rob her of him? Sniffing, Ari looked around and found a box of tissues on the bedstand. She reluctantly released Rafe's hand and blew her nose several times. Something told her to stay with Rafe. Morgan had asked the doctors to waive the five-minute limit. He'd told them that Ari was engaged to be married to Rafe. It was a white lie, Ari knew, but Morgan had his ways of getting around rules and regulations when necessary, and she was grateful he was here with them.

"Rafe?" she whispered as she came and stood by his bed again. The bars on either side prevented her from sitting down on the edge of the mattress. How badly Ari wanted to slide in on his left side, put her arms around him and just hold him. Hold him and give him her love, her warmth and her undying care.

Unable to do that, Ari gripped his fingers and placed her other hand on his shoulder. She began to pray for his life. Without Rafe's magnificent, vibrant presence, she felt as if someone had torn her heart out of her chest, leaving a gaping, bleeding hole in its place. Trying not to cry, but finding it impossible, Ari bent her head and began to pray in earnest. She knew prayer worked. How often had she seen Inca go to the villages, hold a little baby and by bowing her head and praying, make that baby well again?

There was too much evidence, even among the scientists who often scoffed at such things, to show that prayer always helped an ailing person.

Ari had no idea how long she stood leaning against Rafe's bed praying. She was so deep into her state of compassion and love for Rafe that noises barely intruded into her consciousness. Only when she heard the door open, and the alarmed voices of several nurses did Ari realize something was going on.

"You can't go in there!" one nurse cried. "You're armed! We don't allow anyone with a weapon in this hospital! Maria, call security!"

Blinking, dazed, Ari twisted her head toward the commotion at the door. Her eyes widened.

"Inca!"

Inca smiled grimly, her willow-green eyes glittering. "Ho, little sister." She turned and glared down at the nurse. "This is my brother, *señorita.* Do not call security. I am not here to hurt anyone."

The second nurse, Maria, rushed toward the older, heavier nurse, who had a grip on Inca's arm and was trying to drag her out of the room.

"Juanita! This is the jaguar goddess! Let her go! She can help!"

Juanita instantly released Inca as if her hand had been burned. She gasped. "The jaguar goddess?"

Maria gripped her companion and pulled her farther away from the woman who stood in military garb, her rifle slung over her left shoulder, two bandoleers across her chest. "Aiee, yes! Don't call anyone! She is powerful. No one can hurt her. She is here to help. Don't you see that?''

Inca lifted her chin to an imperious position and looked at Maria. "You are right, *señorita*. Leave us undisturbed, eh? I come to help my brother and his fiancée." Turning, Inca closed the door and looked over at Ari. "I am glad you came back, little sister. Rafe has been waiting for you."

Stunned, Ari stared at Inca, who had clearly come to Rafe's side straight from the jungle. The boots she wore were muddy, and there was mud splattered up the sides of her camouflage trousers. "You heard? Rafe got ambushed at his camp?" Her voice quavered. "They say he'll die, Inca." And she sobbed and pressed her hand against her mouth.

Snorting softly, Inca quickly divested herself of the rifle by propping it against the wall. Ridding herself of the bandoleers, she straightened, threw back her proud shoulders and moved to the opposite side of the bed from where Ari stood.

"Not if I can help it," she muttered, defiance in her low, growling tone.

Ari started to release Rafe's hand.

"No, keep your hand upon him while I examine him," Inca ordered. She frowned and rubbed her hands together rapidly. She then opened them and moved them outwards. Mouth tightening, she cupped her open palms about six inches above Rafe's head.

"What I am doing now, little sister, is feeling the energy from him. My hands become like radar, picking up information," she told her softly as she ran her palms in a circular motion above his head, as if searching for something. Then she moved one hand down the midline of his body. "I know you have come back to tell him of your love. He has been terribly lonely without you. I have watched his spirit flicker a little each day without you being there. He loves you with his being, and that," she said huskily as she looked up and pinned Ari with her gaze, "is what I am hoping will bring him back to us. Now he has a reason to return from the tunnel of light. He has you here, with him."

Ari watched, mesmerized, as Inca outlined every part of Rafe's body, beginning with his head and moving down to the bottom of his blanketed feet. The power throbbing around Inca was palpable.

"You feel so different than before," Ari whispered unsteadily.

Inca smirked, lifted her hands away from Rafe and flung collected energy off them. "That is because, little sister, I am no longer shielding myself, my energy, from you. This is how I normally feel."

"Shielding?" Ari queried. "I don't understand...."
She watched as Inca moved her hands with obvious certainty above Rafe's right side, where his liver was badly damaged.

"Yes. Just as you would turn down the volume of a radio that was playing too loudly because it could hurt your hearing, I shield myself, my energy, who I am, from others because it is unsettling to them."

Inca looked up and withdrew her hands from Rafe's side. "I no longer have to do that with you.

I see you have grown quickly and strongly." She flashed her a smile. "You took me at my word and lived your walk and talk. That is good. Rafe will be very pleasantly surprised by you, by what you have become."

Ari heard another commotion at the door. She twisted around. All five nurses and two doctors, dressed in white uniforms, were pressing against the window to watch what Inca was doing.

"You have an audience."

Snorting, Inca didn't even bother to look up. "Little sister, I want you to very gently place your left hand on Rafe's wound. Put your other hand over his heart. I want you to bend your knees slightly. Keep your feet comfortably apart so that as you stand, you are balanced. When I invoke and ask for my jaguar guide to send his energy through to Rafe, you must be strong. Whatever you feel, whatever you hear or see, do not become frightened and jerk your hands away from him." Inca drilled her with a narrowed look. "This is very important, Ari. I need your love, your commitment to Rafe, in order to talk him into coming back to us. If you jerk your hand away, the connection I and my guide forge will be broken and lost forever. We have only one chance, my sister. One chance…"

Gulping, her heart beating wildly in her chest, Ari did as Inca told her. "I won't let go, Inca. I swear I won't. I love him too much…I want him back…. Please, anything you or your helpers can do…I'd be so grateful…."

Inca settled her right hand over the top of Rafe's head. She placed her left hand over Ari's, which was pressing upon his chest over his heart. "I know you love him. I knew that from the beginning." She smiled a wolfish smile, her eyes glittering as she held Ari's tear-filled ones. "Allow all your love, all your hopes and dreams, to flow into him now. When a spirit hovers in the tunnel between life and death, many times they have to make a choice to stay or go—and it is *their* choice, not ours. If you see Rafe, talk to him. Talk to him as if he were awake and here with us. Do you understand?"

Caught within the throbbing, swirling power that she felt building around Inca, Ari nodded, her mouth dry. "Yes. I won't run, Inca. I swear it."

Taking a deep breath into her body, Inca closed her eyes. "Then let us begin, little sister. We are going to ask for his life, for his spirit, to return to us, to stay. To love you as I know he does... Close your eyes, take a deep breath. Do not open your eyes until I tell you to."

Inca's low, growling words were lost in a jolt of electricity that surged through Ari. Shocked by the wild, powerful tingling now racing through her hands and up her arms, she instantly felt fear. Following Inca's instructions, Ari closed her eyes. Her breath was ragged with fear, with anticipation. She felt a deep burning sensation where Inca's hand rested on hers. Ari almost wanted to jerk her hand from beneath Inca's, but she knew better. Her hand was throbbing as if it were red-hot. That energy quickly raced up both her arms to her head, and she suddenly felt dizzy. With her feet planted apart, her knees bent, she was able to maintain her stance. If she hadn't been prepared for it, Ari would have fallen to the right, as if suffering from a severe case of vertigo.

The electrical energy suddenly left her head and she felt her body explode with a burning, tingling sensation. In moments, Ari had lost all touch with the outer world. All sounds disappeared. Was this what infants and children and the elderly experienced when Inca laid her hands on them? Ari had heard the villagers try to describe what Inca had done to them and they often compared the experience to that of lightning from the sky. Well, it was true, Ari thought.

She tried to hold on to her center, to her emotions, to the fact that she loved Rafe.

Yes, Inca told her, *narrow your focus, your life, your breathing, to your heart, to how you feel about him. Do not waiver. Do not lose that focus. Hold it… That is good.*

Inca's voice rolled inside her head. Ari was so shaken she nearly opened her eyes, but didn't. She remembered Rafe telling her that Inca had the capacity to use mental telepathy. Before, Inca had never unveiled her abilities to Ari like this. Probably because Ari would have run off like a screaming, frightened child. She was no longer a child, she was an adult. Ari realized in those blistering, heated seconds, as the temperature soared through her body, out her hands and into Rafe's quiet form, that she had grown from being a girl into a woman those months in Amazonia with Rafe. He had allowed her the beauty of becoming her own woman. As Ari stood there, she felt herself begin to rock slightly back and forth in sync with the energy that was moving in hot, undulating waves through her and into Rafe.

Suddenly white, bursting light exploded inside of Ari's head. She gasped audibly, but she was so gripped by what she saw, she did not hear the sound she made. Suddenly, somehow, she was standing in a huge, lighted tunnel. Ahead of her was Rafe. The emotions she felt were not hers, but his. Trying to adjust to the situation, Ari felt herself running forward, her arms open, crying out his name. He was standing on the threshold, and she saw several figures made of light hovering nearby, on the other side of that golden line that was like a demarcation between this world and the other. Ari had no idea how she knew that, only that she did.

As she cried out his name, Rafe turned. He was dressed in his usual khaki trousers and short-sleeved shirt. Startled, Ari realized he wasn't wounded at all. He was his normal, vibrant, handsome self. As she ran toward him, her arms open wide, she saw the sadness on his face disappear.

Ari! You're here…how?

Ari felt every nuance of his emotions throughout her entire body, moving into her open heart, which was pounding in her breast. She realized she could talk to him with her mind. She didn't need to speak to him verbally.

Rafe! Come back! Please come back. I need you...I love you! You can't leave me now. I came back to see what we had together. Please, can't you return so we can try to live together? Darling, I love you. I've come home...."

She saw his dark brown eyes lighten to that wonderful cinnamon color. Sunlight sparkled in the depths of his gaze as his mouth lifted into a dazzling smile of welcome. He looked over at the beings of light, then down at the golden line between him and them. Turning, he lifted his eyes to Ari and he laughed. It was the laugh of a man who had been given everything he could have possibly wished for.

Come here, mi flor. *All I want to do is hold you. I love you. I've always loved you. Come here....* And he walked toward her, his arms opening.

Ari cried out his name and flung herself into his awaiting arms. The instant their bodies met and touched, a powerful, shaking bolt of what could only be described as lightning slammed through them simultaneously. Ari cried out and clung to Rafe. She felt them spinning madly around and around. She felt Rafe clutching her.

Don't let go of him!

Inca's growl reverberated through Ari. She clung even more tightly to Rafe as they became spinning light, like a huge, oblong cocoon of glowing energy. She felt movement, but she was unsure of direction. All she knew, all she felt, was a powerful spinning.

Moments later, the light was gone and she was plunged into blackness. She could no longer see Rafe, but she could feel him gripping her hard against his entire body as they were whirled wildly into the inky depths.

Ari felt her fingers loosening behind Rafe's back as the spinning quickened and became more powerful. She felt her arms slipping from around his torso. Crying out, she tried to retain her hold.

Hold him! Do not let him go!

Sobbing, Ari tried. She felt herself being torn away from Rafe. No! She had to struggle. She had to try and keep hold of him, for she knew if she didn't, he would die. Having no idea how she knew that, Ari tried to focus on her heart, on her love for Rafe.

Yes! Concentrate! Empower yourself! You can do this!

Strengthened by Inca's growling voice hurtling around in her head, Ari inched her fingers back around Rafe's torso. There! She locked her hands behind him. The blackness was complete. She felt as if she were being swallowed up.

Then, just as suddenly, there was a jolt, as if a jet flying at Mach 3 had slammed into a steel wall. Ari gasped. Light and color splashed violently up around her. She felt herself being ripped away from Rafe. Oh, no! And then she felt herself falling...her knees buckling and her body meeting the cold linoleum of the hospital floor with a thud.

* * *

Ari groaned. Her lashes fluttered open. Where was she? What had happened? She saw Inca leaning over her, her green eyes narrowed upon her. She felt the woman warrior's hand gently caressing the top of her head.

"You will be fine, my brave little sister." Her lips curved and she showed her even, white teeth. Looking up, she nodded toward the bed where Rafe lay. "And thanks to you, so will he. Come, get up. You will be weak now, but you will be fine in a few hours."

As Ari clung to Inca's strong arm and got to her feet, she saw the stunned expression of the nurses and doctors who were standing outside the room, faces pressed to the glass. Dizzy, she put her hand to her brow.

"I felt like I just got hit by a Mack truck," she muttered.

Chuckling deeply, Inca took her over to Rafe. "Here, hold on to the rail for a few minutes. Spread your feet and keep your knees soft. The energy will run out of you and you will feel better."

Instantly, Ari forgot her own confusion and instability. "Rafe? How is he?"

Inca moved confidently around to the other side of the bed. She grinned. "Look at his color. You see? Life is flooding back into his face. Pick up his hand. Is it not warmer now?"

Excitement and hope threaded through Ari. Inca was right; there was a dull flush to Rafe's cheeks as he lay there unmoving. Gripping his fingers, Ari found them warm and alive once again.

"He is returning, little sister. Look..." Inca pointed to his fluttering lashes. "Welcome him home, eh? You were responsible for him returning to us."

Without thinking, Ari leaned over the bed and pressed her lips against his parted ones. No longer were they cool. Tenderly, she moved her mouth against his. She breathed her life into him. As he took a deep, shaking breath, she felt tears slide down her face. And when he exhaled, she drank his breath deep into her body, and into her heart.

Easing her lips away from his, she whispered, "Come back, Rafe. I'm here. So is Inca. I love you, darling. I love you with every cell of my being. Please, open your eyes. We're here. We're waiting for you...."

Ari had no idea where her words were coming from. All she knew was that she was speaking from her heart, her soul. Whatever had happened was a miracle, as far as she was concerned, and she realized that even more when Rafe's dark, spiky lashes opened to reveal his cloudy brown eyes. She smiled gently down at him. "Welcome home, darling. I love you. I'll be here with you every step of the way. You're going to live, Rafe. Do you hear me? You're going to live...."

"I think you've upset the hospital personnel by returning from the grave," Ari told Rafe the next day. She'd remained with him throughout the last twenty-four hours, since he'd miraculously emerged from the coma. He was no longer in ICU. They had transferred him to a private room in another wing of the hospital. Rafe was sitting up, pillows behind his back, the pale blue of the cotton pajamas emphasizing his deep, golden skin, which now glowed with returning health. He was still weak, so she guided the glass of orange juice to his lips.

As she sat there helping him, her heart throbbed with such joy that she was unable to understand what had happened. She knew the healing Inca had given him was powerfully catalytic. When the doctors had rushed in shortly afterward to examine Rafe, they'd been stunned. After several more tests with the CAT scan, they'd pronounced his liver not only there, but healthy and no longer shredded or torn by the bullet that had ripped through it.

Inca had placed a kiss on Rafe's brow as the doctors rushed in, said goodbye to Ari and then left, disappearing just as mysteriously as she had appeared. Now Ari wished Inca had remained. She had so many questions to ask her since that profound experience.

Rafe smiled weakly as she eased the glass from his lips. "This is like a dream," he told her, his voice sounding rusty. "I dreamed of you being in the light with me. I knew I was dying. The angels on the other side told me it was my choice as to whether I came back or not...." He slid his hand into hers, her hip resting gently against his thigh as she sat beside him.

"And when you held me, I felt my heart explode with such pain and joy. I thought I was having a heart attack…"

Ari sighed and slid her fingers down his darkly haired arm. "So much happened, Rafe. I'm not sure about all of it, or how to explain it…."

He rested his head against the pillows. "Inca is powerful in many mysterious ways. That is why she's called the jaguar goddess. The people of the Jaguar Clan are all shamans and healers of varying strength and power. She is one of their most powerful."

Chewing on her lower lip as she watched Rafe close his eyes, that tender smile lingering at the sides of his mouth, Ari wondered why she'd ever doubted her love for this man among men. Squeezing his fingers a little, she whispered, "I'm so glad she came. If she hadn't, the doctors gave you less than forty-eight hours to live."

Rafe felt the terror in Ari. Feeling her like this, experiencing her every emotion, was new to him, but he didn't mind it. The healing that Inca had given him must have forged a deeper bond and connection with Ari, one that gave him privileged access to her emotional state. Sometimes he could swear that he could read her mind, too, because he knew what she was going to say before she spoke the words out loud. Squeezing her fingers in turn, he whispered, "Now that I have a good liver, the doctors tell me that in a few days I can go home."

"Home to your house here in Manaus," Ari told

him sternly. "*Not* back to your camp near the Juma Indian village."

Hearing the fear in Ari's voice, he opened his eyes. Right now, all he wanted to do was sleep. He knew a sick animal would curl up, unmoving, and sleep for days. Sleep was the great healer. But before he did, he wanted to reassure Ari. He saw the worry banked in her glorious, light blue eyes. She looked beautiful in her purple floral skirt, alive with pale yellow daisies, pink carnations and deep blue hibiscus. The purple short-sleeved, seed-stitched rayon sweater that she wore with it only emphasized her beauty even more. Love for her swelled through his chest.

"*Mi flor,* we will go to my *casa,* my home, here in Manaus. Don't frown, my love. Right now, it's a time of healing, of celebration, because we're together once again." Closing his eyes, Rafe felt himself being pulled into a very deep, healing sleep. The fact that Ari was here, had spoken of her love for him, was all Rafe needed. The future was uncertain in some ways. He wanted only the peace and quiet that his home—which stood on the edge of Manaus with the walls of the jungle surrounding it—could provide. He saw his home as their castle where they could finally be alone and in complete privacy with one another. Rafe eagerly looked forward to that day. It couldn't come soon enough....

Chapter Twelve

Rafe wandered across the red tile patio that adjoined his house, which stood next to the green wall of the rain forest. It was fall now, March, and he could see the change in the birds that were on their migratory travels northward, where spring was just about to occur. Hesitating midway across the wide expanse, Rafe stopped and observed Ari.

She sat at the wooden picnic table where she always drew her orchids since coming to live and take care of him in the aftermath of his gunshot wound. Several bright ceramic containers in front of her held the rainbow array of pencils. She sat looking out upon the rolling green lawn and the rain forest beyond. Sunlight slanted in beneath the protective Spanish tile roof, the rays touching her hair, which hung in golden strands around her shoulders as she worked.

This morning was warmer than usual. A sluggish, humid breeze moved slowly across the open patio. He smiled a little as he watched her work with confidence. How much Ari had changed in the eleven months he'd known her. There had been a shift of balance and energy between them since his wounding. Ari moved with new certainty and confidence, and she had nursed him back to full health. No small thanks to Inca, either, who had come once a month to lay her hands on his healing liver, too. Just yesterday, the doctors had given him a clean bill of health. They said it was a miracle he was alive, and that his liver was fully functioning now—as if he'd never been injured in the first place. Rafe had grinned knowingly into their confused faces. For years, he'd seen the power of the Jaguar Clan at work on his people, the Indians of Amazonia. Little did he know that he would need their services, too. He had much to thank Inca for.

Gazing around, he eyed the large wooden trellises on either side of the patio, each covered with a profusion of climbing flowers. Bougainvillea was thorny, but gorgeous. The white, vibrant violet and fuschia colors were like splashes of paint from a master's brush. He watched with joy as a great egret landed on the lawn to look for frogs that weren't already hibernating for the coming winter season. He saw Ari stop her work, lay down her pencils and simply take time to watch the tall, graceful white bird walk across the recently mowed lawn.

Rafe didn't want to spoil the moment. He clasped the small, dark green velvet box in his left hand, feeling fear. Anticipation. Hope. Anxiety. What would Ari say to his proposal? Was it too soon? In his country, a woman was courted for at least a year, and then a man could ask for her hand in marriage. Would Ari say yes? Rafe was uncertain. She *seemed* happy with him here in Manaus. The rift with her father had been healed to a great extent. Ben Worthington had flown down for a visit a month ago. Luckily, Rafe had gotten along well with him. Ari's father had looked him over closely, as if evaluating whether or not his daughter deserved better than him. In the end, Ben gave them his blessing, much to Ari's relief.

Frowning, Rafe stood and watched Ari's changing expressions as she enjoyed the visit of the white heron. When Worthington found out that Ari had her own bedroom, and that nothing was going on between her and Rafe, he'd lost a lot of his anger and aggressiveness. One day after Ben was unduly harsh with Ari, Rafe had taken him aside and told him that if he couldn't treat his daughter with the respect she deserved, he could leave the country now. At that moment, Ben Worthington changed his attitude toward Rafe. Ben was a man who respected power, and when Rafe challenged him one-on-one, man-to-man, Worthington's esteem for him rose. Ben demanded to know his intentions toward his daughter.

Rafe told him he was going to ask for her hand in marriage as soon as he felt the moment was right. When Rafe asked if Ben had a problem with that, Worthington had sputtered, his face turning a dull shade of red. He'd said that he didn't particularly like the idea of his daughter living in the rain forest. He didn't want to see her put in danger as Rafe had been when he was shot and nearly killed in the line of duty.

Rafe smiled slightly now as the egret walked on yellow stilt-like legs toward the red tile path that led up to the porch. He saw the quiet happiness on Ari's rapt features as she watched the proud bird move with dignity and grace. As he gazed at Ari, his mind drifted back to the confrontation with Worthington. Ben had challenged him about what he would do to keep Ari safe if she decided to marry him and live in Brazil. Rafe had been thinking a lot about that on his own and he discussed some ideas he had with the man. If the cocaine factories of the valleys to the north of his camp could be destroyed, and the Valentino Brothers put out of business, the bulk of the murdering and kidnapping in his region would end.

Worthington gave him a wolf smile over his statement and told him that a top-secret project, which had been years in the planning, was about to occur. The Brazilian government was going to team up with the U.S. and go after the very cocaine factories Rafe spoke about. Worthington, in his position in the Pentagon, had supported this eradication mission from the start. The fact that he didn't want his only re-

maining daughter out in the rain forest hunting for
orchids one day, only to be snatched away by drug
lords and placed into chains to work in a cocaine
factory, made him even more supportive of the plan
to go forward. Rafe was shocked by the news, but
grateful, for it answered his concerns for Ari's safety.
Worthington said that the selection of people to work
with the Brazilian government was occurring as he
spoke.

Knowing that, Rafe promised Ari's father he
would not take her to his encampment near the Juma
village until the joint mission had been launched and
was successful. He would go down five days a week
and return home to Manaus—and her—on week-
ends, until the balance of power in the basin was
changed with military might. Ben had said that was
reasonable. He'd shaken Rafe's hand and said that
he'd come down to Manaus with a lot of prejudice
toward Rafe, but after meeting him, he could see the
possibility of Ari marrying him.

Having Worthington's blessing helped, Rafe
thought, feeling somewhat more at ease about the
proposal he was about to make. He watched as the
egret suddenly spread her three-foot wings and lifted
off the grassy lawn, obviously startled by Rafe's approach.

"I think he saw me coming," he called to Ari, so
he didn't frighten her as well.

"Rafe!" Ari twisted around. "Where have you
been?"

He smiled tenderly and sat beside her. "Busy,"

he told her enigmatically, holding the jewelry box between his hands. "How is the drawing going?" He gazed at the pure white orchid with a purple spotted lip that she had sitting on the table in front of her.

"Fine." Ari brushed some tendrils of hair away from her cheek as the sluggish breeze moved through the patio. They had shared lunch out here two hours ago. Usually Rafe puttered around in the small garden nearby pulling weeds, or he sometimes took a walk into the rain forest to simply commune with nature. She reached out and touched his shaved jaw. "So, what have you been up to? You look like the cat that caught the canary."

He looked down at his hands. "I can't fool you, can I, *mi flor?*"

Ari slid her arm across his shoulders and leaned against his tall, strong frame. "Not often," she admitted. "What are you hiding in your hands?"

His heart raced a little to underscore the sudden anxiety he felt as her fingertips brushed his closed hands. Turning to her, he slid his left arm around her, their knees touching. "A gift for you, Ari. At least, I hope you see it as a gift...."

As Rafe met and held her gaze, Ari saw such tenderness burning in the depths of his cinnamon-colored eyes that her breath hitched momentarily. She saw the nervousness in the line of his full, strong mouth, in the perspiration dotting his brow.

"A gift?" she whispered excitedly. "But you've given me so many already, Rafe!"

That was true. He showered her with small gifts.
Oh, they didn't cost money, because on his salary he
could not buy her expensive things. No, he looked
for ways, daily, to tell her of his love for her. Sometimes it was a new orchid that he would receive from
one of the tug captains who plied the Amazon River.
Other times, he would cut flowers from the garden,
put them in a vase in her bedroom and wait for her
to discover them. Some days, he would make her
favorite breakfast, quiche with spinach and bacon.
Or her favorite dessert, butterscotch pudding.

"You are a gift to me," he told her in a low,
serious tone. He watched her eyes widen beautifully
and her pink lips part. "And I was thinking, while
standing and watching you and the egret, of how
much of a miracle you are in my life, Ari. How
much—" he swept his hand toward his humble
house "—the past three months have meant to me."
He sobered and looked down at her. "I hope they
have been happy months for you as they have for
me."

Touched, she leaned her brow against his shoulder, her hand resting on his hairy forearm. "I've
never been happier, Rafe. You know that. Even after
the shock of finding out my father had hired you to
protect me I forgave you and him. I understand why
you did it."

He slid his hand across her jaw and eased it up so
that her gaze met his, then he smiled a little. "I'm
glad I agreed to be your guard dog." Then, becoming more serious, he whispered, "I don't take what

we share for granted, *mi flor*. Every day I wake up and you are here is a miracle come true for me.'' Releasing her chin, he held up the velvet box.

"And because you are the miracle in my life, I'm asking for your hand in marriage.'' He opened the box with some difficulty, his hand shaking slightly. As he opened it, he heard Ari gasp.

Her hand flew to her mouth. There on the green velvet sat a gold ring with seven small, faceted blue-green stones. "Oh, Rafe...'' she cried softly.

"It's aquamarine, from a mine north of here. The finest gemstone in the world.'' He touched the stones carefully. "I wanted a wedding ring that reminded me of the beautiful color of your eyes, *mi flor*. In your eyes, I see hope. I see happiness with you.'' Choking, he rasped, "And I hope you see the same when you look at me.'' Picking up the delicate ring, he held it out to her and asked, "Ari, will you marry me? Will you be my wife? The mother of our children, who will be welcomed with love between us?'' He anxiously searched her face, his heart pounding in his chest.

Tears stung her eyes. Her hands fell away from her mouth and her fingers closed around his and the ring he held out to her. There was such trepidation in Rafe's moist eyes. Shaken, she touched the ring. "This is so wonderful, Rafe. Yes...a hundred times yes, I'll marry you!'' she sobbed.

Relief sheeted through him. He closed his eyes momentarily, his anxiety turning to an avalanche of joy. "Here, let me see if it fits correctly,'' he said, taking her left hand and gently easing the aqua-marine ring onto her finger.

Her flesh tingled wildly as he eased the ring into place. Ari couldn't believe her ears. But her heart believed. She desperately loved Rafe. She knew the custom of his country was to be formal about engagements and marriage. And even more wonderful, Rafe would be able to announce the engagement to his family, as he and his father had found peace between them. When Sebastian Antonio had gotten word that his son lay dying in the ICU of a Manaus hospital, both he and his wife had rushed to his side. Ari had been there to see the tearful, happy reunion. By that time, Rafe had been healed and was recovering wonderfully. Ari had been privy to the moment when Rafe's father apologized and told Rafe he was no longer disowned, that he wanted his son back as a member of the family. Everyone had cried that morning, even Ari.

Gazing up at Rafe now, her smile soft, she held her hand up with the ring glinting upon it. "It's so beautiful, Rafe. I love it...." She reached out and slid her hands around his thick, powerful shoulders. "And I love you...with all my life, with every breath I take, my darling...."

Her words were like sunlight enveloping him. Rafe allowed her wobbling words to sink into his consciousness. The tears in her eyes were real. With his thumbs, he eased the moisture away from her flushed cheeks. "I love you with my heart, my soul, my beautiful flower woman...." And he did. Still he was surprised when, moments later, Ari fluidly rose to her feet and gripped his hand.

"Come with me? To my bedroom? I want to love you, Rafe. I want to show you how much you mean to me." Ari wasn't sure he would say yes. Rafe had been so proper, so careful not to pressure her. Oh, they had shared warm, wonderful kisses and touching, but he never allowed his hands to stray to her breasts or anywhere else that was intimate or provocative. Ari knew that women saved themselves for marriage in South America. There was a wonderful anticipation in waiting, and now, as she stared down at him, smiling tenderly, she saw the shock of her words sink into him.

Feeling his fingers tighten momentarily around hers, she heard him ask, "Are you sure, Ari?"

Laughing softly, she answered, "I've never been more sure of anything, darling. I know you wait here in South America." She held the ring up to him. "But we're going to get married. And as scared as I am because I haven't much experience in loving a man, I want you lying beside me. I want your arms around me. I want to follow our kisses and see where they lead us."

Rising to his full height, Rafe caressed her flaming cheek. "There's no need to be afraid or unsure, *mi flor*. Just let your heart guide you and everything else will unfold like a blossom on a newly born flower...."

Within moments they were in Ari's large, spacious bedroom. The furniture was made of bamboo, the

cushions brightly colored flower patterns. Ari especially loved the large, queen-size bed with the head
and footboards made of gnarled liana vines that Rafe
had cut and crafted. As they walked into her room,
the mid-afternoon light making everything gauzy in
appearance, Ari sat down on the thin quilt that covered the bed, running her hand lovingly over the fab-
ric as she looked up at Rafe. He had told her that
his grandmother had stitched this quilt fifty years before. He had grown up with it, and his grandmother
used to bundle him up in it and rock him in her arms,
when he was sick or just in need of comfort as a
child. The quilt was composed of flowers that grew
in Brazil. Some of them were orchids.

"I love this quilt," she whispered as she watched
him unbutton his dark green cotton shirt. As he divested himself of it, she stared up at his powerful,
well-sprung chest, which was covered with thick,
black hair. After laying the shirt across one of the
chairs near the foot of the bed, he turned. She saw
the vivid red scar where the surgeons had cut into
his flesh to save his life. Now Rafe was as stalwart
and strong as when she'd first met him.

"It is a quilt filled with ageless love," he agreed
in a deep voice. Unbuckling his belt and opening his
trousers, he eased them off his legs. Ari's expression
told him what to do next. Placing the trousers on the
back of the chair, he approached her and eased her
on to her back. "And loving you here is something
I've dreamed of for so long," he whispered. How
easy it was to slip each shell button through its but-

tonhole and open her pink cashmere sweater to reveal the white silk camisole beneath. Ari wore no bra. She never had, and Rafe applauded her stance. A woman's breasts were naturally beautiful and needed no confining. That, in his mind, was taming the innate wildness of a woman. He wanted his woman natural and free. As he removed the sweater he trailed his fingers to the thin straps of her camisole. "Loving you," he said darkly as he drew up the satiny garment and slipped it over her head, "is a miracle to me...."

Ari sighed as the silken edges of the camisole skimmed her breasts. Her nipples hardened in anticipation. She thought she'd feel embarrassed being undressed by Rafe, but just the opposite occurred. She slipped off her shoes and lay there as he eased her dark blue slacks away from her hips, down her knees and away from her feet. She closed her eyes, wanting only to feel his touch. It was butterfly light. The warmth and hardness of his thigh against hers as he leaned over her made her sigh with anticipation. Whatever fear and anxiousness she'd had before disappeared as she felt his roughened fingertips outline her collarbone.

"You are so beautiful," Rafe whispered as he moved onto the bed with her and uncoiled his length against her. The golden color of his skin beside her pale, white flesh shouted of their differences. And yet, as he watched her lashes close and her lips softly part when he began to touch her, worship her, there really wasn't any difference between them at all.

Leaning over, he allowed his hand to trail languidly
from her shapely collarbone and follow the curve of
her flesh, the crescent of her small, upturned breast.
As he closed his lips around the tight peak, he felt
her arch and moan. Instantly, her hands slid up his
arms, her fingers digging convulsively into his flesh.
She tasted of life as he suckled her, first one nipple
and then the other. Her moans of pleasure resonated
through him and he smiled to himself. More than
anything, Rafe wanted to please her, to initiate her
and welcome her into the realm of his love for her.
Never had he wanted a woman to be more satisfied
than Ari.

The moments became molten for Ari. She was
nearly helpless to do much of anything as Rafe performed his tender assault upon her senses. His fingers skimmed her tightening flesh, cupping her
breasts and leisurely moving down her rib cage to
flow across her slightly raised abdomen and then tan-
talizingly brush that most sacred, secret place between her taut thighs. As his mouth took hers, she
leaned up, her fingers digging deeply into his shoulders. Her breathing was ragged. Her heart beat like
a bird's wings in a sudden flurry of flight. And when
he slipped his hand between her thighs and asked
her to part them, to trust him, the heat, the sliding
friction, of his fingers finding the moistness of her
womanhood, exploded within Ari.

All sounds ceased to exist except his roughened
breathing, the thunderous pounding of his heart
pressing against her tightened breast. As his fingers

hotly teased her, she cried out beneath his mouth, a cry of absolute pleasure from the velvet explosions taking place without warning deep within her body. Her skin was damp. She was hungry for him in ways she had never experienced. As if sensing this, Rafe eased himself on top of her, and gently nudged her with his knee, asking her to open herself fully to him.

She absorbed the feeling of his muscular bulk across her. As she slid her arms around his powerful shoulders, she felt him asking entrance. Opening her eyes, she saw the agony in his narrowed gaze. His nostrils were flared. He was gritting his teeth and controlling himself for her. All those realizations struck her, and Ari smiled softly up at him and moved her hips upward to meet and pull him into her. The sensation of pressure, heat and pleasure combined, and her lashes closed. A gasp tore from her lips as he eased into her, taking her and making her his. His hands moved beneath her shoulder blades and he thrust deeply into her at the same moment she arched her hips to receive him joyfully within herself.

The greatest gift Ari could give him was all of herself. All the power of the sunset moments, the moonlit nights, the rolling thunderstorms that she had experienced here, at his home, occurred explosively within her as he began to rock her, thrust deeply into her and brand her with himself, his essence as a powerful masculine animal. As she clung to his mouth, which took hers with relentless enjoyment, as she rocked with him in the primal rhythm,

Ari began to understand the richness of being more animal than thinking human being. The odor of his flesh made her lick the perspiration from his shoulder. And when she teethed his shoulder, he groaned. Little by little, she released her human side and became more the raw, unfettered animal in his arms. His male scent intoxicated her. He tasted strong, and she cherished his mouth with a wild abandon, giving and taking with the same primitive joy that fueled a wild new rhythm.

She was a part of nature—of the rain forest, the damp, decomposing earth, the life-giving rain that splattered across the triple canopy. Part of the howl of the monkeys, the call of the rainbow-colored toucans and the sunlight thrusting through the clouds. She was all of those things as she felt her body become a volcano of swelling, building lava. And when the explosion tunneled through her, she gave a breathless cry of surprise and clung to Rafe as he thrust harder and deeper into her, to give her the pleasure, the gift of his sensual, primal lovemaking.

The world, the scents and fragrances, the feel of his longer, powerful body protectively covering hers, all melted together in a collage of pleasure that Ari had never before experienced. If she'd ever doubted what desire was, she knew now. When she felt him tense, and heard a low, guttural growl thunder from his chest, from his drawn-back lips, she moved her hips intuitively and created an equal pleasure for him as he released his life deep within her.

The moments afterward left Ari feeling weak but

satisfied. Rafe moved off her and bundled her into his arms, his hand sliding deliciously down the long curve of her back in a reverent gesture. He kissed her damp brow, her closed eyes and the corners of her smiling mouth. She lay in his arms feeling loved, protected and cherished. How wonderful it was to love and be loved by him. Her mind refused to think coherently. Ari didn't care. When Rafe's mouth lingered like honey on her lips, she tasted him with her tongue.

"My flower is really a jaguar in disguise," he said with a chuckle near her ear. Indeed, Ari's wildness had surprised him, but it was a gift to Rafe. As he lay on his side, with Ari in his arms, her body pressed languidly against his all the way to her delicate toes, he smiled. Her eyes were barely open, her cheeks a rosy hue. Her mouth, that delicious part of her, was wet and gleaming from his kisses, his adoration of her.

"Mmm, well, it takes one to know one," she sighed. Running her hand across his chest, she let her fingers tangle in the damp strands of dark hair. "I love you, Rafe Antonio." Ari met his dark, stormy gaze. "I love you with every breath I take or ever will take." Sobering, Ari slid her hand across his damp jaw and felt the stubble of his beard. Her skin tingled wildly. "I've never felt like I do now...."

Rafe nodded. "My body sings with yours. We were meant for one another, my beautiful flower." He eased several blond strands of hair away from her damp, flushed cheek. "The music we make is our own. The voice, the sound our bodies make with one another is simply a miracle, *mi flor.*"

With each tender stroke of his hand across her cheek, her brow and her hair, Ari absorbed him like he was the sun and she the orchid below, reaching for the life-giving energy. "You're my sunlight. Did you know that?"

He chuckled again and his hand came to rest upon her hip. "No, but I like the idea of it." Gazing deeply into her lustrous, pale blue eyes, he whispered, "You are my flower. I am your sun. Surely we will care well for one another, my woman." He eased his hands down across her abdomen. "Perhaps we will have children who will be like small orchids, who will grow between us and with us. You are the life-giving water, I am their sun."

Nodding, Ari snuggled her brow beneath the line of his jaw. "Life with you will never be dull, Rafe. And I'm sure that if we're meant to have children, they will be raised in the wilds of Amazonia." She curved her fingers against the hard muscles of his forearm. "I can't think of a better place to raise children than here. They'll discover life in all its fullness and beauty. We love Amazonia. We love the life in her." With a contented sigh, Ari whispered, "Oh, Rafe, I'm so happy. I think I'm going to explode."

His mouth pulled back in pleasure. "We'll explode together, okay?" Moving his hand languidly across her damp flesh, he looked up and studied the gauzy ambiance of the sunlit room. He had in his arms the woman he'd loved since setting eyes upon her eleven months earlier. They had each gone through their own private challenges and hells. And they'd emerged victorious because of the love they held for one another.

Rafe didn't fool himself; he knew there was danger in his work, and that Ari needed protection. As he closed his arms more surely around her, he sighed. Life was a cycle, he reminded himself. They had gone through hell for one another and this was the reward. There would be many other challenges, but together, they could surmount them. As long as they had love, nothing was impossible.

As he lay there with Ari in his arms, the sunlight now shooting through the feminine lace at the open window, Rafe smiled softly. Sleep was nearby. He was fully satiated and fulfilled. The woman he loved was here, at his side. How much Ari had grown and flourished as a woman since he'd met her. He liked her newfound boldness, her certainty in who and what she was becoming. Rafe was going to enjoy watching her continue to unfold like the mysterious orchid she was. What a miracle that was to him: to watch her gain confidence, to change, to reach out regardless of fear, and to keep moving forward.

All these things she was experiencing now would be passed on to their children. His smile deepened as sleep's wings moved across him. Ari was his. He was hers. And he would love her—forever.

* * * * *

Attention Lindsay McKenna Fans!

MORGAN'S MERCENARIES

*continues next month, with a
brand-new romantic adventure:*

MORGAN'S MERCENARIES:

HEART OF THE WARRIOR

*Don't miss Inca's much-antcipated
romance with Roan Storm Walker, a
mercenary who proves more than
worthy of this spirited woman's
love and passion!*

*Look for this longer length,
single title volume at your favourite
retail outlet!*

Turn the page for a sneak preview.

Inca was lonely. Frowning, she shifted her position on the large wooden crate where she sat, her booted feet dangling and barely touching the dry red soil of the Amazon's bank. Sighing, she looked around in the humid, midafternoon haze.

She wondered why she felt so lonely. Ordinarily, she didn't have to deal with such emotions. She was so busy most of the time she could block out the more tender feelings that sometimes wound around her heart like a vine. But not today.

Today she had to meet the man her blood brother, Michael Houston, had told her she must work with on her next mission.

Her lips, full and soft, moved into a grimace. She had a mild curiosity about this man called Roan Storm Walker. The fact that he was part Indian made her feel better. Indians shared a common blood. Inca wondered if the blood that pumped through Walker's veins was similar to hers.

Shrugging aside thoughts of this man, Inca eased a plastic bag out of the pouch she wore and gently opened it. Inside was a color photo of Michael and Anne Houston. In Anne's arms was six-month-old Catherine. Inca hungrily studied the photo, the edges frayed and well-worn from being lovingly looked at by her so many times in quiet moments. Michael and Anne had named her Catherine's godmother. Inca finally had a family.

Pain moved briefly through her heart. Abandoned at birth, Inca had only bits and pieces of memories of her childhood. In the first sixteen years of her life, she had been passed from village to village, having many mothers and fathers. Why had her real parents abandoned her? Had she been a bad baby? Looking at the photo of Catherine, who was a chubby-cheeked, wide-eyed, happy little tyke, Inca wondered if the reason her parents had left her out in the rain forest to die was because she had been so ugly at birth. Whatever the reason, the pain of abandonment was always with her.

He's coming.

Instantly, Inca placed the photo back in the pro-tective plastic covering and into the pouch at her side, sensing that the man known as Storm Walker would be arriving shortly. Standing, Inca felt her heart pound a little harder as she saw the yellow-and-black taxi roaring over the crest of the hill. Eyes narrowing, Inca saw the shadow of a large man in the back seat. Wrapping her arms against her chest, she waited tensely. There weren't many people Inca trusted, and she had no reason to trust this stranger entering her life.

The cab screeched to a halt and she watched a very tall, well-built man emerge from the back of the vehicle. As he straightened, Inca's heartbeat soared. He looked directly at her across the distance that separated them. Her lips parted. She felt the intense heat of his cursory inspection of her. The meeting of their eyes was brief, but it branded Inca.

As the man leaned over to pay the driver, Inca felt a warm sheet of energy wrapping around her. Startled, she shook off the feeling. What was this? Inca afraid? Oh, yes, fear lived in her. But she knew fear was not a reason to quit.

Inca watched as the man leaned down and captured two canvas bags in his grip before turning to face her. He was taller than she'd expected. Automatically, she lifted her strong chin, met his assessing cobalt-colored eyes and stood her ground.

His face was broad, with a hooked nose like an eagle, a generous mouth and many tiny lines around the corners of his eyes. His hair was black with blue highlights, close cropped to his head, typical of the military style, she supposed. He wasn't wearing military clothes, however, just a threadbare pair of jeans, hiking boots and a dark maroon polo shirt that showed off his barrel chest to advantage.

This was not the lazy *norteamericano* Inca was

used to seeing. No, this man was hard-bodied from hard work. His biceps were thick, the corded muscles of his forearms distinct. There was a tight coil of energy around him as he moved slowly toward her, his gaze locked with hers.

Inca dug her gaze mercilessly into his eyes, looking for his weaknesses, for that was what she had to do in order to survive—find the enemy's weakness and use it against him.

Instinctively, she knew it was the only way she'd make it through this mission with the man they called Roan Storm Walker....

www.eHarlequin.com

MAITLAND MATERNITY

Where the luckiest babies are born!

Join Harlequin® and Silhouette® for a special 12-book series about the world-renowned Maitland Maternity Clinic, owned and operated by the prominent Maitland family of Austin, Texas, where romances are born, secrets are revealed…and bundles of joy are delivered!

Look for

MAITLAND MATERNITY

titles at your favorite retail outlet, starting in August 2000

HARLEQUIN®
Makes any time special ™

Silhouette®
Where love comes alive ™

Visit us at www.eHarlequin.com　　　PHMMBWIBC

Coming soon from

Silhouette® SPECIAL EDITION®

**An absorbing new miniseries from
bestselling author**

GINNA GRAY

A Family Bond

Bound by brotherhood...fueled by desire!

Three strong, smolderingly sexy heroes embark on an
emotional search to unite their long-lost family. In their
quest for belonging, what Matt, J.T. and Zach discover
along the way will test their courage and alter their lives
forever. And it will take three very special ladies to tame
these dynamic siblings with soul-searing kisses and
tender promises of true love....

A MAN APART
(SE#1330, on sale June 2000)

IN SEARCH OF DREAMS
(SE#1340, on sale August 2000)

THE TIES THAT BIND
(Coming in fall of 2001)

Available at your favorite retail outlet.

Silhouette®

Where love comes alive™

Visit Silhouette at www.eHarlequin.com   SSEAFB

Coming Soon
Silhouette Books presents

Weddings in White

(on sale September 2000)

A 3-in-1 keepsake collection
by international bestselling author

DIANA PALMER

Three heart-stoppingly handsome bachelors are paired
up with three innocent beauties who long to marry the
men of their dreams. This dazzling collection showcases
the enchanting characters and searing passion that
has made Diana Palmer a legendary talent
in the romance industry.

Unlikely Lover:

Can a feisty secretary and a gruff oilman fight
the true course of love?

The Princess Bride:

For better, for worse, starry-eyed Tiffany Blair captivated
Kingman Marshall's iron-clad heart....

Callaghan's Bride:

Callaghan Hart swore marriage was for fools—until
Tess Brady branded him with her sweetly seductive kisses!

Available at your favorite retail outlet.

Silhouette®

Where love comes alive™

Visit Silhouette at www.eHarlequin.com   PSWIW

If you enjoyed what you just read,
then we've got an offer you can't resist!

Take 2 bestselling
love stories FREE!
Plus get a FREE surprise gift!

Clip this page and mail it to Silhouette Reader Service™

IN U.S.A.
3010 Walden Ave.
P.O. Box 1867
Buffalo, N.Y. 14240-1867

IN CANADA
P.O. Box 609
Fort Erie, Ontario
L2A 5X3

YES! Please send me 2 free Silhouette Special Edition® novels and my free surprise gift. Then send me 6 brand-new novels every month, which I will receive months before they're available in stores. In the U.S.A., bill me at the bargain price of $3.80 plus 25¢ delivery per book and applicable sales tax, if any*. In Canada, bill me at the bargain price of $4.21 plus 25¢ delivery per book and applicable taxes**. That's the complete price and a savings of at least 10% off the cover prices—what a great deal! I understand that accepting the 2 free books and gift places me under no obligation ever to buy any books. I can always return a shipment and cancel at any time. Even if I never buy another book from Silhouette, the 2 free books and gift are mine to keep forever. So why not take us up on our invitation. You'll be glad you did!

235 SEN C224
335 SEN C225

Name	(PLEASE PRINT)	
Address	Apt.#	
City	State/Prov.	Zip/Postal Code

* Terms and prices subject to change without notice. Sales tax applicable in N.Y.
** Canadian residents will be charged applicable provincial taxes and GST.
  All orders subject to approval. Offer limited to one per household.
  ® are registered trademarks of Harlequin Enterprises Limited.

SPED00   ©1998 Harlequin Enterprises Limited

Beloved author

JOAN ELLIOTT PICKART

reprises her successful miniseries

THE BABY BET

with the following delightful stories:

On sale June 2000
TO A MACALLISTER BORN
Silhouette Special Edition® #1329

The Bachelor Bet's Jennifer Mackane proves more than
a match for marriage-wary Jack MacAllister.

On Sale July 2000
THE BABY BET: HIS SECRET SON
Silhouette Books®

A secret son stirs up trouble for patriarch
Robert MacAllister and the clan.

On sale October 2000
BABY: MACALLISTER-MADE
Silhouette Desire® #1326

A night of passion has bachelor Richard MacAllister awaiting
the next bouncing MacAllister bundle!

And coming to Special Edition® in 2001:
HER LITTLE SECRET.

Available at your favorite retail outlet.

Silhouette®

Where love comes alive™

Visit Silhouette at www.eHarlequin.com   PSBET

Silhouette®SPECIAL EDITION®

presents an exciting new miniseries by

PATRICIA McLINN

WHERE WYOMING HEARTS BEAT TRUE...

On sale August 2000—
LOST-AND-FOUND GROOM
(SE#1344)

On sale September 2000—
AT THE HEART'S COMMAND
(SE#1350)

On sale October 2000—
HIDDEN IN A HEARTBEAT
(SE#1355)

Available at your favorite retail outlet.

Where love comes alive™

Visit Silhouette at www.eHarlequin.com   SEAPCH

Attention Silhouette Readers:

Romance is just one click away!

online book **serials**

➤ *Exclusive* to our web site, get caught up in both
  the daily and weekly online installments of new
  romance stories.

➤ Try the Writing Round Robin. Contribute a chapter
  to a story created by our members. Plus, winners
  will get prizes.

romantic **travel**

➤ Want to know where the best place to kiss
  in New York City is, or which restaurant in
  Los Angeles is the most romantic? Check
  out our Romantic Hot Spots for the scoop.

➤ Share your travel tips and stories with us on
  the romantic travel message boards.

romantic reading **library**

➤ Relax as you read our collection of Romantic
  Poetry.

➤ Take a peek at the Top 10 Most Romantic Lines!

Visit us online at

www.eHarlequin.com

on Women.com Networks

SEUT1

Silhouette®

SPECIAL EDITION®

COMING NEXT MONTH